Barry Gifford was born in 1946, in Chicago, Illinois. He has been the recipient of awards fr or the Arts, the Art Director n Library Association. His n award-winning film by D n Francisco Bay Area.

By the same author

Fiction

Francis Goes to the Seashore
Landscape with Traveler: The Pillow Book of Francis Reeves
A Boy's Novel
An Unfortunate Woman
Wild at Heart: The Story of Sailor and Lula
The Wild Life of Sailor and Lula
Port Tropique
New Mysteries of Paris

Non-fiction

A Day at the Races: The Education of a Racetracker
The Devil Thumbs a Ride & Other Unforgettable Films
The Neighborhood of Baseball
Saroyan: A Biography (with Lawrence Lee)
Jack's Book: An Oral Biography of Jack Kerouac
(with Lawrence Lee)

Poetry

Ghosts No Horse Can Carry: Collected Poems 1967–1987
Giotto's Circle
Beautiful Phantoms: Selected Poems
Persimmons: Poems for Paintings
The Boy You Have Always Loved
Selected Poems of Francis Jammes
(translations with Bettina Dickie)
Coyote Tantras
The Blood of the Parade

BARRY GIFFORD

59° and Raining

The Story of Perdita Durango

Paladin
An Imprint of HarperCollins*Publishers*

Paladin
An Imprint of HarperCollins*Publishers*
77–85 Fulham Palace Road,
Hammersmith, London W6 8JB

Published simultaneously in hardcover
and paperback by Paladin 1992

First published by
Random House Inc. New York 1991
9 8 7 6 5 4 3 2 1

A catalogue record for this book
is available from the British Library

ISBN 0 586 09188 2
0 586 09189 0 (paperback)

Set in Baskerville

Printed in Great Britain by
HarperCollinsManufacturing Glasgow

This book is dedicated
to the memory of Larry Lee
1942–1990

'Pleasure which vanishes vanishes for good . . .
Other pleasures come, which replace nothing.'

Roland Barthes

Contents

Fast Forward 11
Sisterhood 13
The Name of Science 15
The Good Life 17
Night Thoughts 19
New Morning 20
Letter from Caribe 22
Travel Plans 24
Local Color 26
The Cause 27
The Hand 29
Desperado 31
Pigeons 33
Faces 36
A Few Good Men 38
Storm Warning 40
Bad Road 42
Heroes 44
The Bat 46
Pleasures 48
Beauties 49
Il Affare 51
The House of Dreams 55
Quiet Time at the Rancho Negrita Infante 57
The Other Side of the River 59
Good Eye 62
Tough Boys 65
Bon Voyage 67
Ghouls 70
Lives of the Saints 73
Communion 76
The World and Everything in It 78
The Big Day 80
A Visit to Sparky & Buddy's 83
Critics 86
The Choice 88
Rubout 91
Out of the Past 94
Detour 95
Flight 100
Salamanders 102
History Lesson 105
Back at the Nursery 107
Waves 110
Camisado 113
After Hours 116
Late Date 119
Light in the Forest 120
The Old Testament 121
Back from Eternity 122
59° and Raining in Tupelo 123

Fast Forward

Perdita met Manny Flynn in the San Antonio airport restaurant and bar. He was gobbling chicken fajitas and she was smoking a cigarette, an empty glass in front of her on the table, which was next to his.

'You wanna 'nother one?' Manny asked.

Perdita looked at him. Fat but neat. He wiped his thin lavender lips with a napkin. A waitress came over.

'Sweetheart, bring me another Bud and give that girl there whatever she wants.'

'Wish somebody'd make me an offer like that,' said the waitress. 'What'll it be, honey?'

Perdita took a long drag on her Marlboro, blew out the smoke and killed it in an ashtray.

'Coke,' she said.

'Diet?'

'Not hardly.'

The waitress looked hard at Perdita for a moment, then wrote on Manny Flynn's check.

'One Bud, one Coke,' she said, and hurried away.

Manny forked down the last bite of fajita, wiped his mouth again with the napkin, stood up and redeposited himself at Perdita's table.

'You live in San Antone?' he asked.

'Not really.'

'You sure do have beautiful black hair. See my reflection in it just about.'

Perdita withdrew another Marlboro from the pack on the table and lit it with a pink and black zebra-striped Bic.

'You catchin' or waitin' on one?' asked Manny.

'One what?'

'A plane. You headin' out somewhere?'

'My flight's been cancelled.'

'Where you lookin' to go?'

'Nowhere now. About yourself?'

'Phoenix. Four-day computer convention. I sell software. By the way, my name is Manny Flynn. Half Jewish, half Irish. What's yours?'

The waitress brought their drinks, set them down quickly on the table without looking at Perdita, and left.

'Perdita Durango. Half Tex, half Mex.'

Manny laughed, picked up his beer and drank straight from the bottle.

'Pretty name for a pretty Miss. It *is* Miss, isn't it?'

Perdita looked directly into Manny Flynn's eyes and said, 'You want me to come to Phoenix with you? You pay my way, buy my meals, bring me back. I'll keep your dick hard for four days. While you're at the convention, I'll do some business, too. Plenty of guys at the hotel, right? Fifty bucks a pop for showin' tit and milkin' the cow. Quick and clean. You take half off each trick. How about it?'

Manny put the bottle back down on the table, then picked it up again and took a swig. Perdita turned away and puffed on her cigarette.

'I gotta go,' Manny said. He threw several bills on the table. 'That'll cover mine and yours.'

He stood and picked up a briefcase and walked away. The waitress came over.

'I'm goin' off duty now,' she said to Perdita. 'You finished here?'

Perdita looked at her. The waitress was about forty-five, tall and skinny with bad teeth and phony red hair that was all kinked up so that it resembled a Brillo pad. She wore one ring, a black cameo with an ivory scorpion on the third finger of her right hand. Perdita wondered what her tattoos looked like.

'Just about,' said Perdita.

The waitress scooped up Manny Flynn's money. Perdita nodded at it.

'Gentleman said for you to keep the change.'

'Obliged,' said the waitress.

Perdita sat and smoked her Marlboro until the ash was down almost to the filter.

'Dumb cocksucker,' she said, and dropped the butt into the Coke.

'Mummy says he has more money than he knows what to do with.'

'Why does he work, then? He still works, doesn't he?'

'Oh, he's just so greedy, that's why. Mummy says he needs to work just to have something to do, which doesn't make any sense at all. At least not to me. I mean, he has all kinds of stocks and everything, lots of property all over the country. He's just so cheap I can't stand it, and neither can Mummy.'

'So why does she go out with him?'

'It's just someone, I suppose, until she can find a man she really likes. Could be he's hung like an Australian crocodile, for all I know. Mummy's always had a weakness for big cocks. She told me.'

'She told you that? My mother's always acted like babies come from a stork.'

'You mean like dropped down a chimney?'

'Yeah, I guess.'

Both girls laughed.

'She'd never talk to me about sex. Once I asked her if they had Tampons when she was a girl and she said, "When the time comes, young lady, we'll discuss all that sort of thing." Then, when I got my period in March, remember? The week before my birthday?'

'I remember.'

'She gave me a box of Kotex sanitary napkins and a can of cunt spray and said, "More of each of these will be on the second shelf of your bathroom closet."'

'So she never discussed anything?'

'Get real. My mother would drop dead if she knew half of what I've done.'

'Mine, too, probably, even though she's such a slut herself.'

'Come on, I need to get some boots to go with that cowgirl skirt Kristin gave me.'

'Sounds good. Oh, do you have your credit cards? Mummy took mine away for a month and I might see something I like.'

'Yeah, no prob.'

Perdita watched the two girls as they walked out of the coffee shop. Neither of them was more than twelve years old. Both had long blond hair, wore tight, short, black skirts, expensive-looking blouses and large gold hoop earrings. Perdita felt for a moment like stabbing them each in the back and chest and throat dozens of times. She imagined their blood running black, dripping down their smooth golden legs. Just as suddenly the feeling passed, and she forgot about them.

That evening, when Perdita was driving along Tres Sueños, she saw two little girls, eight or nine years old, sitting on the lowered tailgate of a parked pickup truck, petting a fuzzy brown puppy. One of the little girls had long, dark hair cut into bangs in front; she reminded Perdita of herself when she was that age. This sight made Perdita sad because it made her think also of her twin sister, Juana, who was dead. Juana had been shot and killed by her husband, Tony, who was drunk, during an argument. Tony had then murdered his and Juana's two daughters before putting the gun in his own mouth and blowing off the top of his skull. Perdita missed Juana, and her nieces, Consuelo and Concha, too. She guessed she might forever. Tony she always could have lived without.

The Name of Science

When Perdita first saw Romeo Dolorosa she thought he was very ugly. He was drinking a papaya milkshake at an outdoor fruitstand on Magazine Street in New Orleans. She ordered a large orange juice and avoided looking at him, staring across the street at a Shoetown. When she turned back to pay, the fruitstand operator, a bent-backed, dark gray man of indeterminate age or race, said, 'The gentleman there already done, sweet thing.'

'It's your lucky day, señorita,' said Romeo. 'And mine, perhaps, too.'

'What's that supposed to mean?' asked Perdita. 'I don't need a new friend.'

Romeo laughed. 'Oh, but you do,' he said, and laughed again. 'What a charming manner you have, Señorita Spitfire. Are you the daughter of Lupe Velez? My name is Romeo Dolorosa.'

Perdita looked more closely at Romeo. He was really quite handsome, she realized, with long, wavy black hair, deep brown skin and blue eyes; perhaps an inch under six feet tall, but substantial looking. He had beautifully shaped, very muscular arms that tapered gracefully down from the short sleeves of his blue and red Hawaiian shirt. It was odd, Perdita thought, that her first impression of him was so unflattering. She wondered what she had seen in Romeo to have made him appear that way.

'I don't know what you're talking about,' she said. 'Thank you for the orange juice. My name is Perdita Durango. Who is Lupe Velez?'

'Better, much better. Lupe Velez was an actress, a movie star from Mexico sixty years ago, who was famous for her hot temper.'

'Why should I have reminded you of her? You don't know me.'

'I am trying to make a beginning. Please, I apologize for my presumptuous behavior. Do you live in New Orleans, Perdita?'

'I've only arrived this afternoon. I'm looking around.'

Romeo nodded and smiled broadly. He had very large white teeth.

'If you will allow me to buy you dinner,' he said, 'I'll be happy to show you the town.'

As Perdita sipped the orange juice through a straw, she raised her 8-ball black eyes to Romeo's, smiled, and nodded slowly.

'Now we're getting somewhere,' he said.

At Mosca's that evening, Romeo asked Perdita if she knew what a 'resurrection man' was. She shook her head no.

'A hundred years ago and more,' said Romeo, 'doctors at medical colleges paid men to rob graves, mostly in nigger cemeteries, and deliver the corpses to them to be used for dissection by students. The doctors soaked the bodies in whisky to preserve them. It wasn't until almost the twentieth century that laws were changed to permit dissection of humans.'

'Why you tellin' me this?' asked Perdita, licking salad dressing off her fork.

Romeo grinned. 'Science is everything,' he said. 'The most important thing, anyway. Often it's necessary to go against what is the popular thinking to achieve discoveries. I think about things this way, scientifically. There's nothing I would not do for science.'

'About those people saw the Virgin Mary at Tickfaw?' asked Perdita. 'And the woman in Lubbock took the photo of St Peter at the gates of heaven? How's science deal with that?'

'Need funds to research,' Romeo said. 'Like the $1,925 some fundraiser withdrew without permission this morning from the First National Bank of St Bernard's Parish on Friscoville Street in Arabi. Science needs money, just like everything else.'

'You tellin' me you're a grave robber or a bank robber? I ain't totally clear.'

Romeo laughed and stuck a fork into his stuffed catfish.

'Scientists gotta eat, too,' he said.

The Good Life

'I knew a guy once named Bobby Peru,' said Perdita. 'You know, like the country? Thought he was a bad dude, and he was, kinda. Coulda helped us out here, I think, but he got himself killed.'

'Know what soothes me?' Romeo said.

Perdita laughed. 'Yeah, I sure do.'

'That, too,' said Romeo. 'But I like to read the weather reports in the newspaper. Like for other places than where I am. "Ten below with snow flurries in Kankakee." "Fifty-nine and raining in Tupelo." Never fails. Calms me.'

Perdita Durango and Romeo Dolorosa were sitting facing each other in a bathtub filled with smoky gray warm water in the Del Rio Ramada. Romeo was fondling an H. Upmann New Yorker and flicking the ash into the bathwater.

'Wish you wouldn't do that,' said Perdita.

Romeo laughed. 'Why not? Keeps away the evil spirits, don't it?' He laughed again, showing off his perfect Burt Lancaster teeth.

'How long you suppose these guys are gonna go for this voodoo shit, Romeo? They ain't all all the way stupid.'

'Makes you say that? Could they might be. Besides, it ain't voodoo, neither. *Santería, chiquita*. That's hocuspocus, Latin-style. But you're right, we gotta do somethin's gonna make 'em pay better attention.'

'I know what'll do it,' Perdita said.

'Yeah?'

Perdita nodded, her thin black eyebrows uncoiling like cobras. 'Kill somebody and eat him.'

'You mean like cannibals.'

'Sure,' she said. 'Nothin' can be more horrible than that. It'll stick in their brain.'

Romeo laughed and puffed on his cigar.

'You bet it will, OK,' he said. 'Stick to their ribs, too.'

Perdita smiled and tickled Romeo's penis under the water with the big toe of her right foot. The cobras on her forehead flattened out like reptiles on a rock in the sun.

'You know how to help a man in both mind *and* body, *mi corazón*. What I like about you. It's the good life, OK.'

'Let's do it tomorrow,' Perdita said.

Night Thoughts

At three-thirty in the morning Romeo woke up and lit the half of the cigar he'd left in the ashtray on the table next to the bed. The smoke woke Perdita up.

'What's the matter, hon?' she said. 'Can't sleep?'

'Thinkin'.'

'Anything in particular?'

Perdita had her eyes closed; her long black hair was strewn across her face.

'Once read about how just before the Civil War ended, rebel soldiers buried the treasury of the Confederacy within one hundred paces of the railroad tracks between McLeansville and Burlington, North Carolina.'

'How come nobody's dug it up?'

'Good question. It was all gold coins kept in iron cooking pots. Some farmer found one of 'em, but there's supposed to be about fifty million dollars' worth still in the ground there. Somethin' to think about.'

'For after we get done here, maybe.'

Perdita fell back asleep. Romeo finished off most of the Upmann, imagining himself overseeing a crew of his disciples digging up pots of gold along a stretch of railroad tracks next to a tobacco field. The disciples could then be shot and buried in the holes. This was not impossible, he decided.

New Morning

Perdita woke up and turned on the radio. She lay in bed listening to the news with her eyes closed.

'Finally,' said the broadcaster, 'from China today comes the announcement that seventeen convicted felons were sentenced to death and executed before a crowd of thirty thousand people at a stadium in the southern city of Guangzhou. The public trials and executions were carried out, according to the *Legal Daily* newspaper, "in order to allow the masses to celebrate a stable Chinese Lunar New Year." How's that for Southern justice, folks?'

Perdita switched it off. She looked over at Romeo, who was still asleep. His mouth was open and his mustache drooped over his upper lip, the long black hairs fluttering as he snored. Romeo might be part Chinese, thought Perdita. The way his face hairs hung so limp, not like on Mexicans. Or Spanish, she reminded herself. Romeo insisted on identifying himself as Spanish, no belly-crawling Indian blood in his veins. Perdita snickered. No matter what Romeo said, he didn't look like no white man. He even talked like a Chinaman sometimes, so fast you couldn't follow what he was saying.

They were heading back to the ranch today, which was good. She needed to build a new altar for the sacrifice. This would be something different, really special. Not like with the chickens and goats or dogs. Romeo was a good organizer, he knew how to get the shit across the border, how to get the money. Perdita smiled, thinking about the one time Romeo had tried to smoke marijuana himself. He'd gotten dizzy and had to lie down until his head cleared. Wouldn't touch the stuff for nothing now. That was cool, though, she figured. The dope didn't get in the way of doing business. Perdita made a mental note to buy more candles, they were almost out. Also some grain alcohol. They could use a new sledgehammer, too.

Perdita stuck the index finger of her right hand into Romeo's mouth and pushed down on his tongue. He gagged, coughed hard, and sat up.

'What!? What the fuck?' he said, and worked at clearing his throat.

'*Vámonos*,' said Perdita. 'We got lots to do today.'

Letter from Caribe

Caribe 2.14.1989

Hello Romeo.

Jest these few lines to let you know that everything at your house is fine. Well Mr Dolorosa sir there is a tolk out in Caribe that you wants to sell your house. People had been asking me about the sale on the house but all I can do is to gave them your phone number so that they can call you and talk with you about it. Well I hope that you will bee back some day jest so that the people wood stop tolking so much shit. Mr Romeo this time I had seed some bad days because in December my dorie brook down cood not even get out to fish can't fine no woor here and most of the time I wood only eat one male per day. So last month the lady at Caribe Keys that bys the fish seant me up her boat so that I can make some money but the first week out fishing was good but the monny was so small. She gets half of the monny an the other half is in between me and another. Look the first 4 days we sold 1,500 Caribe dollar and so far we cant get out for the winds the winds has been from 10 to 20 knots from the eastnortheast an from east for allmost two months that my boddy can get out to fish. I had been a little sick the last pass few week so I went to an Amarican docter here an he told me that my boddy was ran down a lot so he put me on some toneck a madacen and I feale a little better these last few days. But Nelmy had been on an off with her Hedakes. Well yesterday school open for the kids but Alix had healp us a lot with them gatten them most of what they need. Kenny want even come down so that I can get a few days woor with him I jest dont know watt I will do if this wind dont stop I needs to get out fishing for atlest one more week before you gets here. Mr Rome Nelmy sent to say hello an she hopes that you is fine an she wants you to tell Perdi hello for her. And not to forget her T-V. Mr Dolorosa sir I dont know for shore but some people was saying that Rocky

James was senten to jail for 20 years an if Reggie San Pedro Sula ever came back to Caribe he wood go to jail for 15 years. Well the people was at first was saying that you and Mr San Pedro Sula wood go to jail when you ever all got back from the USA but Mr Reggie was here about a week ago and he did not have any problem at all. Mr Romeo if I was you I wood keep away from Reggie San Pedro Sula ontell everything is normal again. Virgil Fredrex is a little up set because Woody Hall took all of his stuff out of the room on the hill an carid it down to his house that is about all for know ontell another Mr Rome take good care Love from my hole fam Nelmy Danito Chonge Nansy Branny and my sister an brothers mom & dad Your good fren

Danny Mestiza

Travel Plans

'Do you think some people are born wanting to travel?' Romeo asked. 'Or do you figure it's a kind of thing comes over you?'

'You mean like in the blood,' said Perdita.

'Sorta, yeah.'

They were bouncing along in the Cherokee on the dirt road between Zopilote and Rancho Negrita Infante. Perdita had purchased everything she required in the hardware store in Del Rio and she was excited. Romeo's babbling usually made her uneasy but today she didn't mind listening, giving him the feedback he needed to process his thoughts.

'When I was a kid in Caribe, you know,' he said, 'my family used to go to the harbor when my Uncle Roberto went to sea. I was seven years old the first time I remember it clearly. There was a big gray boat tied up at the dock. "*Margarita Cansino*" was the ship's name, in giant black letters. And underneath that was painted the port of origin, "*Panama*." We were there to hug Tio Roberto and wish him a safe journey, which, of course, I did. But I was so impressed by the size of the ship and the thought of it sailing out into the ocean beyond the Gulf, beyond the Caribbean, that the idea of traveling entered my dreams. From that moment I knew I would voyage out far into the world beyond Caribe.'

Perdita, who was driving, did her best to avoid the ruts and large rocks in the road. She lit a Marlboro with the dash lighter.

'But yet here you are,' she said, 'still not so very far from there.'

'I've come back, of course. After all, this is my home. I told you about when I lived in New York, in Paris, in Los Angeles. I was in Buenos Aires and Montevideo, too. In Caracas, Miami, La Paz. One day I'll go to Egypt, to China, to Madagascar to see the fabulous monkeys. I am already twenty-seven years old, but I have plenty of time to travel. Soon there will be enough money for us to travel whenever and to wherever we want.'

'It makes me happy to have you include me in your plans,' said Perdita.

Romeo laughed. 'And why not? You're the proper one for me. Four years younger, beautiful, smart, strong. Someday we'll have children.'

'You'll inform me, of course, when the time for that is appropriate.'

'Of course, *mi amor*. You'll be the first other than me to know.'

'*Bueno, jefe*. And what other plans do you have for us?'

'It's enough for now to finish this business we have.'

'I've been thinking about it, Romeo. I think what we have to do is take someone off the street. An Anglo.'

Romeo looked at Perdita through his brown-lensed Body Glove glasses.

'An Anglo?' he said.

'That would make the most impression.'

Romeo turned his head and stared out the open window at the desert. The hot breeze caused by the Jeep's passage plastered his black hair to his forehead.

'Kidnapping,' he said.

'What?' said Perdita. 'I couldn't hear you.'

Romeo gritted his teeth and let the wind hit his face. Believe it, he told himself. Life with this woman will be without apologies.

Local Color

Perdita stopped the Cherokee at the entrance to the Rancho Negrita Infante. She cut the engine and got out, leaving the driver's door open. A few feet from the Jeep she squatted, coiled her skirt around her and urinated on the sand. Romeo watched Perdita from the passenger seat and grinned.

'Always liked it that you don't never wear panties,' he said, as Perdita climbed back in.

'Easier that way,' she said. 'Used to I wore 'em, but one day I just left 'em off. Now I don't think I own a pair.'

Perdita started the Jeep up and proceeded toward the complex. She liked this drive, the dust and white sun. It was like being on another planet.

'You know I never asked you,' Perdita said, 'about how the ranch was named.'

'Story is some local woman got pregnant by a black American soldier, and when the child was born it was black, too, a baby girl. So some of the villagers – they're called "*Los Zarrapastrosos*," the ragged ones – took the baby and killed her and buried the body out this way in an unmarked grave.'

'Why'd they do that?'

Romeo shrugged. 'Ashamed, I guess. Surprised they didn't kill the mother also and bury them together.'

Perdita wiped the sweat from above her upper lip and pulled the hair out of her eyes.

'Jesus but I hate that kind of ignorant shit,' she said.

The Cause

There was a main house, a large shack, really, about twenty-five feet by thirty feet, made of tarpaper and wood. The windows were rough squares cut to accommodate removable boards, but they were nailed shut. There was a smokehole above a black cauldron that at the moment contained a boiled hog brain, a turtle shell, a horseshoe, the spinal column of a goat, and dried blood. On the otherwise bare walls were cheap representations of Our Lady of Guadalupe and Jesus Christ. On the floor next to the crudely built altar was a *Book of Rites* from La Iglesia Lukumi Babalu-Aye.

'Leave the door open, honey,' Romeo said to Perdita. 'Get some of the stink out.'

'We have to clean this place up, Romeo. Get your boys in here with some brooms. Dump the garbage. They leave their goddam empty bottles and cans everywhere.'

'*Sí*, señorita. I will see to it immediately.'

Romeo laughed and grabbed Perdita, pulling her to him and kissing her. She shoved him away and began emptying her bags of candles.

'Hey, *santero*, let's do this, OK?'

Romeo and Perdita cleaned up the house themselves, and then Romeo hauled the debris away in the Jeep. He dumped it in a trench his men had dug about a mile away. Gray shit swirled in the brown air. It reminded Romeo of the August day he came back to Tampa after completing the year he'd been stationed in Lebanon with the Marines. Maria-Jose, his grandmother, had asked him, 'They let you visit the Garden of Eden?'

Adolfo Robles drove up in his 1950 Dodge pickup and leaned out the window.

'What we up to, Romeo?' he asked. 'We got something going later?'

Romeo took a black kerchief from his back pocket and wiped the sweat and dirt from his face and neck.

'Something big, Adolfo. Meet me back at the house.'

Adolfo nodded and grinned, jammed the Dodge into gear and drove slowly away. Romeo kicked some dirt into the trench. He'd been one of the lucky ones, having survived the bombing of his Marine barracks in Beirut. More than two hundred sleeping men had died and Romeo had been barely roused by the noise of the explosion. Standing and sweating next to a garbage pit in Mexico, he was convinced there was a noble reason he'd been spared. Romeo pulled out his cock and pissed into the pit. He stood there after he'd finished, fondling himself, watching the steam rise. The air smelled burned.

The Hand

'The island of Petit Caribe, where I was raised,' said Romeo, 'is approximately one mile long and three miles wide. There were only two automobiles on Petit Caribe back then and of course one day they collided with each other.'

Adolfo laughed. 'But how could that happen?' he asked.

'How everything happens, Adolfo. It was in fact impossible for it *not* to happen. This is the working of the world.'

Romeo and Adolfo were sitting on the bottom step of the porch drinking Tecates. Perdita was inside arranging the chairs and candles.

'Look, here is a letter I just received from Caribe, from my cousin, Reggie, who takes care of the old family property.'

Romeo took an envelope out of his back pocket, opened it and removed a piece of paper. 'Listen,' he said.

'"*Dear Cousin Romeo. I hope this Letter finds you doing the verry bes for your self. I talked to your Lawer on how much it would cost to bring the people to move the two men on the land and he Said 3000 Caribe dollar he mus be out of his mind I then call the Aterny Generald office to my fren Teresa. She is the secon to the Boss. Teresa said nothing can be done so I took the mater in my owne hand and the problem is solve. The only thing is to tell you the sharks are have a feaste day. So Good News.*

'"*The weather gets good now I hope we are now in our third week of Bad Weather Romeo. Can you send som monie for fishing wire and the wood turnin lathe an som tools an som buckets also sheet rock screws. I am try to buy a mud Hog pump too for workin the Swamp Land joining the North Line by Rockys property. My daughter Halcyan almos drown in the Lagoon las week but she is fon now. All we here wish you well an you send us som thing now OK? Your cousin an pal – Reggie.*"

'There are constant difficulties on the island,' said Romeo, 'the same as anywhere. There is no more sense made there than here.

You must control your own hand, Adolfo, remember! The rest is unimportant.'

Adolfo nodded and studied his left hand. After a few seconds he drained the Tecate and, with his right hand, tossed the can as far as he could.

Desperado

'I had a friend in Tampa a few years ago,' Romeo told Adolfo as they rode in the Dodge truck toward the border. 'Eddie Reyes, a Cuban from Marianao. He lived for a while with my family, even after I left there. I don't know where he is now. Eddie had been a cop but quit the force and was going to law school at night when I met him. He worked during the day in a meat packing plant.

'This Eddie would take several showers each day, very long showers during which he would scrub himself all over many times and use great quantities of soap and shampoo. Then he would spend an equal amount of time drying himself. Eddie had much hair on his body and lots of curly black hair on his head, and of course he had a beard. I do not exaggerate when I tell you that this bathing and drying process took up most of his time.'

Alfonso, who was driving, shook his head and laughed.

'He sounds like a crazy man,' he said.

'Yes, he was probably a little crazy,' said Romeo, 'but let me tell you why. One night when Eddie was a cop he was sent to investigate a burglary in progress and a junkie got the drop on him. The junkie made Eddie lie down on the ground on his back and stuck the dangerous end of a forty-five automatic between his eyes. The junkie told Eddie he was going to kill him and pulled the trigger. Eddie shit and pissed in his pants and the gun jammed. The backup cops arrived and the junkie panicked, dropped the forty-five on Eddie's chest and tried to run but the other cops caught him.

'The junkie never went to jail. He gave the cops some information they needed about some other scam and he was allowed to plead guilty to a charge of firing a weapon in a public place. Even though the gun never went off! He got away with a suspended sentence. When Eddie heard about it he quit the force and got the job in the meat packing plant. Eventually he started taking law courses. I always figured all the washing he did was connected to the junkie trying to shoot him. It made Eddie a little strange, I guess, still trying to clean off the shit and piss.'

'Maybe it would have been better if the gun had not jammed,' said Alfonso. 'It must be difficult to live in such a desperate way.'

Romeo stared out the window at the passing desert. There was nothing moving other than the heat waves.

'Maybe,' he said, 'but still, it's better to be desperate than dead.'

Pigeons

Perdita and Romeo watched the people pass. They sat at a table behind the front window of the South Texas Barbecue, drinking Lone Star. Perdita's idea was to identify a likely prospect, follow him and in some way lure him back to the Rancho Negrita Infante.

'What are you gonna say, honey?' asked Romeo. 'Come with me to the Casbah?' He laughed. 'We ain't exactly Charles Boyer and Hedy Lamarr, you know. Or, I tell you everything you ever want to know about Lukumi Babalu-Aye? Introduce yourself as a Python Priestess of *Palo Mayombé* and you'd appreciate his allowin' Adolfo to lop off his head with a machete so's we can drain the blood from his body, then hack it apart, cook it up and serve him at the Zombie Jamboree?'

Perdita puffed desultorily at a Marlboro.

'Better you point, I'll follow, club him down, dump him in the Jeep and take off. No tricks.'

'That's a nice one,' said Perdita, pointing to a young guy crossing the street toward them. 'Blond, tan, good shoulders.'

'You gonna fuck him or eat him?'

Perdita raised a cobra eyebrow. 'Both, maybe.'

'He's not alone,' said Romeo. 'There's a girl with him.'

'Could be we'll both get lucky, *macho*. Let's go.'

Romeo and Perdita got into the Cherokee and cruised slowly along the Boulevard Botánica, keeping a close eye on the young couple, who were taking in the tacky bordertown sights.

'College kids,' Romeo said. 'Down from Austin, or maybe just Southmost.'

The couple went into a bar and Romeo parked the Cherokee in front of it. When the couple didn't come out after ten minutes, Perdita said, 'Let's go inside.'

The place was called El Loco's Round-Up, and the young

couple, along with several other people, were gathered around a tall, white-haired gringo who was leaning against the bar and talking. Romeo and Perdita went over to listen.

'Everybody who becomes involved with the movie business learns about it the hard way,' said the man. He looked familiar to Romeo, but he couldn't quite place him. 'When I went out to Hollywood I was fresh from my daddy's insurance company,' the man continued, punctuating his speech with sips of J.W. Dant. 'I didn't hardly know which hole a woman peed out of. Pardon me, ladies,' he said, smiling, 'but that's the truth.'

'Who is this guy?' Perdita whispered.

'Ssshh,' said Romeo. 'I know I seen him somewhere.'

'I was a good-lookin' kid in those days, though, the kind they were after, like Coop, McCrea, Johnny Mack, Randy Scott. Didn't matter I was out of a Boston insurance office. I looked the part, so they stuck me on a horse and I fit. I did all right, saved my money and didn't forget everything they taught me at Harvard, just the things I never could remember. Trained me to talk like I was bred to take my meals from a Montana Hereford. Some of the others, though, didn't do so well. Lash was makin' pornos last I heard. At his age it's more a credit than a discredit. And Sunset's a doorman at the Thunderbird in Vegas. Saw him there myself. Duke, of course, you all know what he did. Licked everyone and everything except the Big C. And Randy didn't die broke. Only real mistakes I made was to marry a couple of American women. Shoulda stuck to Mexican and Japanese, or somethin'.'

When the man paused to pour himself a fresh shot and knock it down, Romeo said to Perdita, 'Happy Pard, Protector of the Pecos! That's who he is. Man's a legend.'

'I heard you, pardner,' Hap said, nodding his head at Romeo. 'You're dead right. Made over one hundred westerns before I got my own TV series. They just churned 'em out over at Republic and Monogram. Started the series when I was forty-five, and it ran nine years. Still on in parts of Asia and South America. My real name is Winston Frost, but everybody's called me Hap for so long I finally had it changed legal. The wiseguys even made me sign my IOUs that way!' He laughed. 'That was a mean road for me, folks, that gamblin'. For years I'd bet on anything. Why, I'd wager on which cube of sugar a fly'd land on. I tell you, that Russian sonofabitch, Fyodor Dostoyevsky, had it pegged natural.

Just read that story of his, "The Gambler," and you'll see what I'm gettin' at. Man was the greatest writer ever lived. Had himself the same problem as me.'

'What's he talkin' about?' Perdita whispered.

'Don't matter,' said Romeo. 'There go your pigeons.'

The boy and girl, neither of whom were more than nineteen or twenty, walked out of El Loco's followed closely by Perdita and Romeo. Perdita caught up to the boy on the street and put her arm through his. Romeo came up next to the girl and showed both of them the nose of his .38.

'Amigos,' he said, 'we're goin' for a little ride.'

Faces

'So what is this? Where are you takin' us?'

'Relax, amigo,' Romeo said. 'Just a ride in the country. And hey, *mil gracias*, by the way, for not makin' a fuss back at the border.'

'Said you'd shoot us if we did,' said the girl.

'Now, sweetheart, I might've, that's right. You can't never be certain a man means what he says, but I've always made sure there's plenty of meanin' in my life. Ain't that right, honey?'

Perdita rode shotgun. She didn't answer, remaining stonefaced, thinking about how best to get the job done. Better to kill them before they got to the ranch. But the boy was cute. She could use him, maybe, then kill him. Romeo'd stick his thing in a keyhole if he thought it'd feel good. He could jump the little white whore if he wanted.

'We'll just be *compañeros* now for a while, if it's OK,' said Romeo. 'Now, my name is Romeo and the mystery woman here is Perdita. What can we call you?'

'Don't say anything,' said the girl.

Perdita stuck her head out the window and let the wind blow through her hair. This is the right girl, she thought. They'd snatched them the perfect platinum bitch. Be easy to smack her, that's for sure.

Romeo laughed. 'Better to be friendly, little lady. Easier all the way around.'

'Why should we make anything go easy for you?' the girl said.

'You figurin' on ransomin' us?' the boy asked. 'If you are, my folks don't have much money. Dad manages a Luby's in El Paso. My mom's a typist for a real estate office. Estelle's folks ain't any better off.'

'Estelle?' said Romeo. 'Is that your name, princess? Estelle. Almost like Estrellita, little star. I like that better, much better.

Estrellita! That's what we'll call you. You like that, Perdita?' He laughed. 'And now you, boy. *Cómo se llama?*'

'It's Duane.'

'OK, OK,' said Romeo. 'I'll take it. Regular name for a regular guy. You look like a regular guy, Duane. You *are* regular, aren't you?'

'I guess.'

Romeo smiled his big smile. 'Now, yeah! We all know each other's names, and that's a step. Duane and Estrellita. Romeo and Perdita. Mix 'em any way you choose. Duane and Perdita. Estrellita and Romeo. How about Estrellita and Perdita? There's a pair. Or Romeo and Duane. Ha! There they go, hand in hand, the good little boys. We could do this one up right, use some brainpower.'

'Where are you taking us?' asked Estelle.

'Show you where the people live, Little Star. Be a place to tell about, you get the chance the next family picnic, all the little Estrellitas and Duanes and things are there, drinkin' bug juice, eatin' pie, honeydews. Fourth of July, could be.'

'Only it won't,' said Perdita, not turning around.

Romeo laughed. 'Oh, Duane and Estrellita, you've heard of "voices"? You know, like, from the air, not from a person.'

'Like disembodied?' Duane asked.

'I think so,' said Romeo. 'Not a body, just a voice. Like from God.'

'Yeah?'

'You're gonna hear it.' Romeo turned quickly, looking around at the boy and girl tied up in the back seat.

'Won't be no Fourth of July, baby,' said Perdita. 'No Thanksgivin', neither.'

'How about *Cinco de Mayo*?' Romeo asked.

Perdita smiled at him, showing an even dozen of her tiny white teeth. 'What you think of Christmas in hell, Chico? Think your honeycunt here can handle that?'

Romeo banged the steering wheel with both hands, howled and rocked back and forth as he drove.

'Holiday in hell!' he shouted. 'Happy fuckin'-A holiday! Whew! You make it right, sugar. Make it fuckin'-A, hard-as-a-rock, crazy-baby OK!'

Perdita laughed. 'Well, I guess I love you, too,' she said.

A Few Good Men

Tyrone 'Rip' Ford had been born and raised in Susie, Texas, and in the forty-three years of his existence had never, excepting his time in the service, lived beyond plain sight of the Rio Grande.

Rip became a deputy sheriff of Larry Lee County when he was twenty-one, three years out of high school and three weeks out of the US Army. He became sheriff of Larry Lee County ten years later and had held the job ever since.

Rip Ford's father, Royal Ford, had nicknamed his son after his own paternal grandfather, Colonel Rip Ford, an early member of the Texas Rangers. After rising to the rank of captain in the Rangers, Rip Ford, elevating himself to colonel, had subsequently recruited a fugitive company of men from South Texas to fight under his command during the War Between the States. Composed mostly of wanted men and men considered too old or too young to be conscripted by the Confederate Army, Ford's irregulars united primarily for the purpose of resisting an expected invasion of South Texas by a Union brigade of Negro soldiers.

Colonel Ford's raggedy group maintained a peripatetic camp along the Mexican side of the border, dodging hostile Kickapoos and Apaches and staging supply raids on isolated settlements on both sides of the river. Declared an outlaw by General Robert E. Lee, his followers branded as criminals and lowlifes, the original Rip Ford attempted to construct a deal just prior to the surrender at Appomattox whereby his company would have switched their allegiance to the North and assisted the Union in a campaign against Mexico. This realignment did not come to pass, but Colonel Ford did succeed in acting as agent between Yankee merchant ship owners and Southern cotton growers, convincing the shipping magnates to place their boats under Mexican registry and transport cotton to the fleet of European ships, mainly English, sitting in the Gulf of Mexico and the Caribbean Sea.

Royal Ford had always admired his grandfather's resourcefulness, and hoped his son – whose Christian name, Tyrone, was given him by the boy's mother, Louise, an ardent admirer of the movie star Tyrone Power – would exhibit a similar tenacity and sense of purpose. Royal was killed during a robbery at the Gulf gas station he'd owned and operated in Susie since his discharge from the army following the Second World War. A drifter named Ulysses Neck had shot Royal Ford in the back of the head while Royal lay face down on the floor of the office of his Gulf station. Ulysses Neck had exactly thirty-two dollars and eight cents in his possession when he was apprehended by two Texas Rangers an hour later less than ten miles away in the town of Fort Dudgeon. Neck took his own life that night by hanging himself by a belt from the high bars of his cell in the Larry Lee County jail, the same jail that Royal's son, Rip Ford, now commanded.

Rip had never married. His life was his work; no citizen of Larry Lee County could question Sheriff Ford's dedication. From Fort Dudgeon to Susie to Madre Island, Rip Ford was well-known and, at the very least, grudgingly respected by Anglos and Hispanics alike. Throughout its century-long history, there never had been a permanent black resident of Larry Lee County. Those Negro Yankee troops so feared by Louise Ford's son Tyrone's great-grandfather never did materialize.

The moment Rip Ford learned of the disappearance of the two college students, Duane Orel King and Estelle Kenedy Satisfy, he felt a sharp pain in his lower back.

'What's wrong, Rip?' asked First Deputy Federal Ray Phillips, noticing the sheriff's grimace.

'Like as somethin' just poked me with a pitchfork above the right buttock, Fed,' said Rip. 'Never felt nothin' like it before.'

'Better hope ain't nobody down in the Mud Huts stickin' no pins in a doll got your name on it,' said Federal.

Both men laughed.

'Nothin's happenin'. *Yet!*'

Fed Phillips looked over at the man who said this and ID'ed him. It was Ramon Montana, one of the county's more prominent drunks.

'You can hear me, Señor Fed! You know I mean what I'm sayin' when I say somethin'. I *said*, nothin's happenin'. *Yet!*'

'Heard you, Ramon. Havin' a good weekend already, I can tell.'

Ramon Montana staggered to the curb where he fell on his knees and regurgitated into the gutter. He shook himself like a wet dog, got up, cleared his throat, threw back his shoulders, put one foot in the air as if he were about to climb a flight of stairs, listed to starboard and toppled to the sidewalk.

'C'mon, there, Ramon,' said Fed, helping him back to his feet. 'Let's see we can get you home before you get so scarred up your sister can't recognize you.'

'Ain't *goin'* home!' Ramon shouted. 'Can't make me. My sister's dead, anyhow.'

'Better'n takin' you to jail.'

Ramon grumbled but allowed Fed Phillips to escort him the half-block to his rooming house, where Fed led Ramon up the stairs and in the door.

'On your own, now, *amigo*. Sleep tight.'

'Tell you, Señor Fed, some strange shit goin' on. You see I ain't talkin'. They gonna kill them kids, them *gringos*, the *gringa*. You hear about it, 'member I tell you firs'. Man got the evil eye. Evil eye.'

Fed closed the door and went back to the street. Who's gonna kill what kids? he thought. Fed headed toward El Loco's to see what he could find out.

Over at the jail, Rip Ford sat in his office looking at the picture of Ava Gardner he kept in a plastic frame on his desk. It was a full-face photo taken in 1954 by a Frenchman, Philippe Halsman. Rip knew this because the photographer's name and the date were printed on the back of the picture. It was a postcard, really, but set into the frame like it was made it look proper, as if it were his wife or fiancée. In the picture, Ava Gardner's tousled black hair obscured her right eye, and her full, closed lips were pulled slightly to the right, resulting in something less than a smile. They looked as if they'd been smeared shut with red paint, though the photo was in black and white. It wasn't so much a fuck-me face as a I've-been-there-and-back look, the kind of expression you see only on the most expensive whores. This was Ava at her best, right after *Mogambo*, which Rip had seen as a boy from the balcony of the Joy Rio in El Paso. It was ten o'clock on Saturday night and he stared at Ava Gardner's immutable face, the face of a lifetime a lifetime ago. Rip let the telephone ring for thirty seconds before he picked it up.

Bad Road

As Romeo drove, Estelle Satisfy thought about her mother, Glory Ann Blue Satisfy, and wondered whether she'd ever see her again. Glory Ann had been born and raised in Divine Water, Oklahoma, a place she dearly loved and wished she'd never left. The house on Worth Avenue in Dallas, where Estelle had grown up, never pleased Glory Ann, nor did Dallas. Glory Ann never stopped complaining about the city. 'When I wake up in the mornin',' she'd say to Estelle, 'I like to know who I'm goin' to see that day. There's too many surprises here in the Big D.'

Glory Ann weighed three hundred pounds now. Her husband, Estelle's daddy, Ernest Tubb Satisfy, who'd been named after the famous singer, stood five-feet four and weighed one-hundred-ninety-five. He drove a 7-Up delivery truck and smoked Larks but took only three puffs of each one before putting it out. Ernest Tubb claimed the Larks lost their taste after the first two drags. He took the third one, he said, just to keep proving it to himself.

Estelle remembered her dog, Gopher, who died after he ate an entire extra large anchovy and onion pizza when she was in the seventh grade. Ernest Tubb buried Gopher under the plum tree in the backyard and Estelle still placed flowers on the grave every year on the anniversary of Gopher's death, April fifth. Estelle thought about these and other things that had happened in her life as the Cherokee bounced down a bad road to only the devil knew where.

Romeo, if that really is his name, looks like the devil, thought Estelle. And that Perdita woman looks weird and dangerous, too. I just hope they're not going to kill us, not before I've even got my cherry popped. That'd be a slap and a half, for sure, after all I've done to preserve my chastity. I should have left it to Stubby Marble. Grace Jane says the Marble boys, Eugene and Stubby, do it better than anyone, and I guess to hell she knows. Stubby kept after me the better part of a month before he gave up. Duane now, he acts like he don't care. I don't know, maybe he don't. I wish I knew what's goin' on here, really. I'm just a college girl with a lot of potential in the field of commercial art who ain't never even got laid yet. I know life ain't fair or even supposed to be, but this is somethin' different.

Duane pretended to be asleep. He kept his head down and tried hard not to think, but he couldn't help it, the thoughts just kept on coming. This wasn't the end of a good time, it was the beginning of a bad one. If Estelle hadn't insisted on goin' out for a beer, Duane thought, we'd be in our hotel room now and maybe she'd be lettin' me. Be a shame to die havin' been with only one girl, and her just Grace Jane Bobble, who the Marbles nicknamed 'The Wide Missouri' not for no good reason. This gal Perdita is a picture, though. Reminds me of that poisonous snake from South America in the reptile and amphibian book we used in biology, one with the triangle-pointed, yellow-red face and orange ice eyes. She's the type'll bite and once the teeth are sunk you'd have to chop off the head with a hatchet to pry loose.

Duane opened his eyes and looked at Estelle. She had her eyes shut and was biting her lower lip and crying. Duane felt like crying, too, but he didn't. He wouldn't stop himself if he started, but no tears came. Maybe I can figure a way out of this, Duane thought. Estelle would be grateful, I bet, and let me do it. I wonder who done it to her other than the Marbles. They said she was some sweet meat. This life's sure got question marks scattered around like dogshit in a empty lot, the way Daddy says. I guess I ain't been steppin' careful enough.

Heroes

'Tell you who my heroes are, Duane. That way you get a better idea of who I am.'

Romeo and Duane were sitting in chairs on the porch of the main house at Rancho Negrita Infante. Estrellita, as Romeo insisted Estelle be called, was asleep in a locked bedroom. It was almost midnight.

'I on purpose am leavin' your legs free, Duane. Sorry about your hands, though. You tell me if the wire's too tight.'

'No, it ain't.'

'*Bueno, bueno*. We got to keep the blood circulatin'. So here's my list: James Ruppert, George Banks, Howard Unruh, Pat Sherrill, Charles Whitman, R. Gene Simmons, Sr, James Oliver Huberty, and Joseph Wesbecker. Know every name by heart. Recognize any?'

'Don't think so.'

'Not even Whitman?'

Duane shook his head no.

Romeo laughed. 'Guess you don't do so good in history class.'

'Got a B.'

'Maybe they didn't cover this part yet. Here's what these men done. Ruppert killed eleven people, eight of 'em kids, at a Easter Sunday dinner in Ohio. Banks took out twelve, includin' five kids, in Pennsylvania. Unruh shot thirteen people in twelve minutes in Camden, New Jersey. He was somethin' else, too. Said, "I'd've killed a thousand if I'd had enough bullets."

'Sherrill murdered fourteen at a post office in Oklahoma. Simmons, Senior, got fourteen, too, all family members, in Arkansas. Buried a dozen under his house. Huberty slaughtered twenty-one at a McDonald's in San Diego, I believe. Wesbecker shot seven and wounded a bunch in a printing plant in Kentucky. And Whitman, of course, cut down sixteen from the tower on the campus of the University of Texas in Austin. Surprised you ain't heard of him.'

'When did he do it?'

'About 1966, around in there.'

'Before my time.'

'Hell, boy, so was Hitler, and you can't tell me you ain't heard of him!'

'I heard of him.'

'How about Attila the Hun? You heard of him?'

'I guess so. He was some kind of Turk or somethin'.'

'Well, I don't include those guys had armies or other people doin' their killin' for 'em. I just rate the ones take it into their own hands. Also, I don't count the serial murderers, the ones done it over a long, drawn out period of time. It's only the ones just all of a sudden know they can't take no shit no longer and just explode on the world! There's more than those I mentioned but those are right off the top of my head. This kind of thing is a particular study of mine.'

Perdita came out on the porch and rubbed her left thigh against Duane's right arm. She put her left hand into his thick blond hair and rubbed it around.

'You been tellin' the boy a bedtime story, Romeo?' she said.

'Just fillin' in a few holes in Duane's education.'

Perdita smiled. 'I got one or two need fillin', too. You two intellectuals feel like helpin' a lady out?'

The Bat

Romeo unlocked the door to the bedroom and entered. He stood still for a full minute, listening to Estrellita's breathing. There was a shrill, brief whistle each time she exhaled. Romeo closed the door, bolted it, and put the key in his right front pants pocket. He walked to the bed and sat down on the edge. Estrellita had long, honey-brown hair, and Romeo stroked it slowly and softly with his left hand. She stirred slightly and he stopped, allowing her to roll over on her back, her head turned to the right. Her eyelids fluttered and she pursed her full lips, then relaxed again, whistling softly.

'Hey, Little Star,' Romeo whispered. 'Come, Estrellita, *niña*. Romeo *es aquí*.'

She didn't move, and her breathing seemed to cease altogether. Romeo smiled. He knew she had to be awake.

'Little Star, don't pretend,' Romeo said, in a normal voice. 'You can open your eyes. All you'll see is me.'

A rivulet of moonlight squeezed into the room through a crack in the second to the highest board covering the window. Estrellita did not move other than to barely open her left eye. She saw Romeo's face in purple shadow, then closed it again.

'You think I come to harm you, huh?' he said. 'Why would you think so? Your friend, Duane, he's not bein' harmed. He's getting happy, probably, by now.'

'Where is he?' asked Estrellita. 'Is he dead?'

Romeo laughed. 'No, of course not, señorita. He's assisting a damsel in distress. Another fair lady, such as yourself.'

Estrellita turned her face to Romeo and opened both of her eyes. He looked like a giant bat.

'You mean Perdita's got him?' she said.

'Yeah, I suppose that's a good way of puttin' it.'

'She reminds me of a kind of snake.'

Romeo smiled. 'A pretty snake, though.'

'She looks cold.'

Romeo moved closer over Estrellita's body and touched her left cheek with his right hand.

'Estrellita, *mi flora blanca de la noche. Tú es la luz de mi vida.*'

She moved her head and shoulders slightly to the right, away from Romeo's touch.

'Don't be afraid, Little Star. You're safe with me.'

Estrellita started to laugh, then suddenly stopped and began to cry. Romeo watched the tears stream out of Estrellita's eyes and roll down the sides of her face into the pillow. Slowly he bent his head and with his tongue licked the tears from her cheeks. Estrellita couldn't move. It was as if Romeo's gesture paralyzed her and his saliva made her face numb. She'd never felt this way before.

'Close your eyes again, Estrellita, *bonita*,' Romeo said, and kissed her left ear, her honey-colored hair, her left eyebrow, the tip of her nose. 'Romeo is going to take care of you.'

Pleasures

'Well, which one is it gonna be?' asked Romeo. 'You think maybe the boy?'

Perdita kicked at the dirt with one of her rattlesnake-skin boots. A soft wind was blowing from the south and it flicked at the ends of her loose black hair.

'*No sé*, baby. This is a tough one.'

'You sweet on him, huh?'

'Be more fun to keep him around for a while, anyway. How about your little *vaca*, Estrellita?'

Romeo took off his straw Stetson and wiped his thick red-black hair with his left hand. He was sitting on the top rail of the corral fence next to the ceremonial hut. The sun was very strong, as usual, but there was a threat of rain in the air. Perdita leaned against the fence, looking east at the scabrous brown hills.

'She was the real thing, chica, *una virgen*. Bled hot and plenty, like *crème de caramel*.'

Perdita laughed. 'Too bad we didn't know it before. To sacrifice a virgin would have made us some serious *mayombérias*.'

'Maybe better to use a local, is what I'm thinkin' now,' said Romeo. 'Get a kid from Zopilote. Duane and Estrellita might come in handy down the line.'

'Tell Adolfo to be sure to have enough garlic this time.'

Romeo laughed. 'You should have seen his face when I told him how when Satan walked out of the Garden of Eden, garlic sprouted from wherever his left foot hit the ground. Adolfo crossed himself and said, "*Madre de dios, es verdad?*"'

Perdita felt an itch between her legs, reached down with her right hand, balled it into a fist, and rubbed her clit hard.

'You know, Rome,' she said, 'the only two real pleasures left to man on this earth are fucking and killing. When those are gone, *guapito*, so are we.'

Beauties

Rip Ford was in bed with a prostitute named Lupita Luján when Federal Phillips called.

'Sheriff, I'm down here at El Loco's Round-Up. A couple of the boys recognized Romeo Dolorosa, that snakepriest dope dealer from Zopilote, and his girlfriend, The Priestess. Apparently they had a beer or two and suddenly disappeared. Nobody noticed they were gone until they were.'

'That it?'

'So far. Gonna check it out further, see if I can get a fix on if the bastard's runnin' anything through here. Be kinda surprised if he is, seein's how he didn't attempt no disguise or nothin'. And, oh yeah, that old drunk Ramon Montana's talkin' some shit about people killin' a couple Anglos. Might be somethin' to do with Dolorosa since Ramon was carryin' on about a dude with a evil eye. That's *santería* talk.'

'Call me back you hear more.'

'You got it.'

Rip hung up and returned his attentions to Lupita.

'Oh, ho-ney,' she said, 'where you get this scar from on your shoulder?'

'Oil spilt from Psyche's lamp.'

Lupita frowned. 'How a lamp can do this to you?'

'Just teasin', sweetheart. Old bullet wound from Nam. Guess you never heard about how Psyche woke up Cupid the middle of one night when a drop of oil burned his shoulder, and how his mama, Venus, made the poor girl's life a misery.'

Lupita shrugged, rolled over and pulled the sheet up over her short plump body.

'I don't hear about nothin' stuck in this pisshole. Who was this bitch?'

'Psyche?'

'Yeah.'

'The most beautiful female mortal on earth. Stole away her mother-in-law's admirers.'

Lupita snorted. 'No wonder she hated the girl. You know her pretty well, huh?'

'We never exactly met.'

'Then how come you so interested? You lookin' to nail her ass, hey?'

Rip got up and pulled on his pants.

'Time to separate reality from myth, Lupita. *Vámonos*.'

Lupita threw back the sheet and stretched. High on her right thigh was a tattoo of a black scorpion with a red stinger poised to strike, sitting on a purple rose. Written on a blue banner beneath it were the words MALA CHICA.

'She have any kids, this *perfecta*?' asked Lupita.

'Matter of fact, yeah,' Rip said. 'A daughter, named Pleasure.'

Lupita laughed. 'She ever hit the street, she don't need to change it, *es seguro!*'

Il Affare

Romeo listened to the train whistles in the distance. They sounded like wheezes from an organ with a mouse running across the keys. He sat in the driver's seat of the Cherokee, smoking, the windows rolled down, waiting for his cousin, Reggie San Pedro Sula, and Marcello 'Crazy Eyes' Santos. It was almost two o'clock in the morning. The crescent moon lit the desert landscape partially, giving it the feel of a bombsite, twenty years after, the only residents rodents, insects and reptiles.

The deal sounded strange, thought Romeo, but if Santos was involved it would, of necessity, be very profitable. Reggie had worked for Santos before, several times, usually as a shooter. He'd do the job, pick up his money and go back to the islands. The money lasted quite a while in Caribe, but sooner or later he'd need another jolt, and as long as Santos survived there would be work for Reginald San Pedro Sula. Romeo was agreeable to the meet, although this was a slightly unusual procedure in a couple of ways. First, Reggie rarely was involved at the top of a deal; and two, Santos seldom ventured out of his hometown of New Orleans. But Romeo was prepared to listen. He knew when and how to be patient.

Romeo heard the car coming. He tossed away his cigarette and waited, listening for half a minute as the engine noise grew louder. The long, black car pulled off the highway across from Romeo and came to a dusty stop. The motor idled and Reggie got out of the back seat, closed the door behind him, and walked over to Romeo.

'*Hola, primo*,' Reggie said. '*Qué tal?*'

'You tell me,' said Romeo, as they shook hands.

Reggie was very tall, at least four or five inches over six feet, and heavyset. He was about fifty years old, his skin was the color of milk chocolate, and he wore a lavender leisure suit. His bald head reflected the moonlight. It was odd, Romeo thought, for Reggie not to be wearing a porkpie rain hat. In fact, Romeo could not recall a time he'd seen Reggie without a hat, other than when he went to sleep, since he'd lost most of his hair.

'I think I let the man, Señor Santos, tell you himself,' said Reggie. 'It's a good deal, a fair arrangement, you'll see.'

Reggie smiled broadly, revealing his numerous gold teeth.

'There must be some danger in it, though,' said Romeo, 'for him to get you off the island.'

Reggie gave a brief laugh. 'There is usually some danger involved, is there not?' he said. 'Though the man needs me for another matter, for where we are heading from here.'

'I see. And how is everyone back home? Danny Mestiza wrote to me that Rocky James got a double sawbuck in the joint.'

'Oh, yes, but he's out now again. I think for good. There was some irregularity but Señor Santos was able to clear it up for him. Halcyan an' Rigoberto is fine an' healthy. The money you sent helped out very good. I talk very strong about you to Señor Santos so he would consider you for this job.'

'What is the job?'

'You come to the car an' he tell it himself. Remember you don't call him "Crazy Eyes." He don't like it when he see it in the newspaper, how they do just to annoy him.'

Romeo climbed down, walked across the road and got into the back seat of the Mercedes-Benz limousine. Reggie closed the door and stood outside. A soft light was on inside the car. Marcello Santos had a drink in his right hand, three fingers of his favorite single malt Scotch whisky, Glenmorangie. He was wearing a dark gray suit with a blue shirt and a red tie; a pair of black Cole-Haan loafers, with tassels, and red, blue and yellow argyle socks; two-dollar drugstore sunglasses with bright yellow frames; and a large gold or diamond ring on each finger of both hands, excluding his thumbs, one of which was missing. He had a brownish-black, curly toupee glued to his head; some mucilage had trickled onto his forehead and dried there. Santos was sixty-eight years old and had ruled organized crime in the southern and southwestern United States for a quarter-century without ever having been convicted of either a felony or a misdemeanor.

'*Buona notte*, Mr Dolorosa. Romeo,' said Santos, extending his left hand, the one minus a thumb, as would the Pope or a princess. 'Good to see you again.'

Romeo squeezed the fingers.

'It is always my pleasure,' he said.

'This is somewhat of an unusual place to meet, I know, Romeo, but as we are on our way to another meeting, and I hate to fly, I thought it would be the most expedient. I'm glad you could come.'

'It's no problem, Marcello, in any case.'

'*Bene*. Your cousin, Reginald, speaks well of you, you know. He tells me you take care of your family and friends back on the island. It's commendable of you.'

'I do what I can.'

Santos nodded and sipped his Scotch whisky.

'Would you like a drink, Romeo?'

'No, thank you. I am driving, and it's very late.'

'Yes, all right. Here is my proposal. It is very simple. There will be a truck here at this spot forty-eight hours from now, a refrigerated truck, accompanied by a car. The truck will be loaded with human placentas to be used in the cosmetics industry. They are blended in skin creams that some people think can keep them looking young. Maybe it does, maybe not. I don't know. This load must be delivered as soon as possible to a private laboratory in Los Angeles. I would like you to drive the truck there for me. That way I know the shipment will be in good hands. The driver of the truck will turn it over to you, should you decide to do this, and leave in the accompanying automobile. All you have to do is deliver it to the address in Los Angeles that this man will give you. I have ten thousand dollars for you now, in old bills, fifties and hundreds. When you arrive safely in LA, your cousin, Reggie, will be there to give you another ten thousand dollars, also in old bills, and in similar denominations.'

'Why don't you just have Reggie drive the truck?'

'I need him with me for a situation between now and when the delivery must be made. He'll fly to California as soon as this other business is finished. Can you do this?'

Romeo nodded. 'Certainly, Marcello. I am glad to help you however I can.'

Santos took off the cheap yellow sunglasses and looked at Romeo. His eyes were grayish-green with large red pupils that jumped and shimmied like flames. Crazy eyes. Despite himself, Romeo shivered.

'*Bene! Molto bene!*' said Santos, patting Romeo on the knee with the four fingers on his left hand. He put the sunglasses back on and drank the remainder of his whisky.

Santos flipped open a panel in the floor and took out a package and held it out to Romeo.

'*Buona fortuna, amico mio,*' said Santos. 'Remember always that God and I, we both are with you.'

Romeo accepted the package.

'I won't forget,' he said.

The House of Dreams

When Adolfo unlocked the shed door, the boy, even though he was blindfolded, looked up, his head cocked toward the noise. His mouth was gagged with a black rag, his hands tied behind his back and his feet bound together with heavy clothesline. He made no sound.

'*Tiene años?*' asked Romeo.

'*Diez*,' said Adolfo. 'Perdita made the choice.'

'What do you know of his family?'

Adolfo shrugged. 'A poor one, like most of those in Zopilote. He is one of four brothers, I think. Maybe two or three sisters. Perdita said it must be a boy. Maybe they don't even miss him.'

'Is Perdita here?'

Adolfo nodded. 'Preparing for the ceremony.'

'Have you notified the others?'

'Everyone will assemble at ten o'clock. Carlos and Teresa are coming from Mexico City.'

'What about the DeLeon family? And the Acostas?'

'No word from Jorge Acosta, but all of them are notified.'

Romeo turned to go, then looked back at the boy.

'Do you know his name?' he asked.

'He is nothing special. His name is Juan.'

'*Oiga, Juanito*,' said Romeo. 'At ten o'clock tonight you will become immortal. Do you know what that means?'

The boy did not move. Romeo noticed the dark stain that ran all the way down the boy's left pantsleg. In the dirt next to his bare left foot was a wet spot the size of a dinner plate.

'It is no matter,' Romeo said.

'This is something an ordinary man can never know. You will enter the House of Dreams, Juanito, where you will live forever. Your mother and father and sisters and brothers, your grandparents, aunts, uncles, cousins, all you will greet in their dreams. And only you, among them, will be safe.'

Romeo went out and Adolfo followed, closed the door and locked it.

Quiet Time at the Rancho Negrita Infante

'So, it's agreed, then. After this we drive to LA for Santos.'

'I always wanted to see California,' said Perdita.

'Duane and I can take turns drivin' the truck, and you and Estrellita can handle the Cherokee.'

'How soon does Santos want it there?'

'Fast as possible. He's not paying me twenty thousand dollars to stop and take a donkey ride through the Grand Canyon. Get what things you want to take together now and put 'em in the Jeep. I want to be ready to go.'

Perdita was painting her toenails shocking pink. Her cunt itched but she knew Romeo wouldn't fuck her, never before a big show. That's how she thought of it, as a performance, like in the circus. She'd only seen a circus once, when she was six years old in Corpus. It was a small troupe, about a half-dozen wagons; one tent, one ring. They'd had an unusual attraction: an albino tiger. Perdita and her older sister, Juana, had stood in front of the cage and watched the beautiful white beast pace back and forth without stopping. Every thirty seconds or so, the tiger would utter a low growl, a lugubrious, slow rumble that seemed to unravel as it hit the air. This noise, Perdita felt, came from extremely deep within the animal, that he was just waiting for the proper moment to release his real feelings, his frustration and wounded pride. At that time his roar would be so deafening, so powerful that the people within aural reach would be paralyzed by fear, and the giant white cat would pounce on them and eat them up.

For weeks after the circus left town, Perdita had dreamed about the tiger. He would stand over her, straddling her lithe girl's body, then pin her to the ground with his paws, his saliva dripping down on her face, before slowly, carefully taking her head into his huge mouth and crushing it with one big bite. This dream did not frighten Perdita. It gave her a warm feeling. The tiger's mouth, she imagined, would be hot and wet, the enormous teeth, gleaming like polished swords, piercing her skin and bones cleanly, painlessly. And then the tiger would chew her, separating Perdita into smaller and smaller parts, until finally, when the beast had swallowed everything, she would wake up.

Perdita had told this dream to only one person in her life, an old man named Pea Ridge Day, who pumped gas in the Green Ace filling station in Corpus. Perdita and Juana would go there to buy grape NeHi sodas from the machine, and Pea Ridge, who was usually just sitting in his red flamingo chair, would talk to them. He told the girls that people called him Pea Ridge because he'd been born in Pea Ridge, Arkansas, but that his Christian names were Clyde and Henry. He said that when he'd been a younger man he'd pitched in the National League for St Louis, Cincinnati, and Brooklyn, wherever they were. Pea Ridge claimed he'd left a note to his wife and kids thirty years before, saying that he was going off into the Ozarks to commit suicide, but instead he hitchhiked down to Texas, where, as Perdita and Juana could plainly see, he was still very much alive. After Perdita told Pea Ridge Day her dream, he stopped talking to her as much, and one morning, when she and Juana went to the Green Ace station for a grape NeHi, he was gone. Perdita decided that Pea Ridge had probably gone back to Arkansas to see his family before he really died. She never absolutely believed that his disappearance was connected in any way to her having told him her dream, but Perdita decided then and there not to tell anyone else about it just the same.

'That sound all right to you, honey?' Romeo asked.

Perdita blew on her toes.

'You know me, baby. I travel light.'

The Other Side of the River

'We live on one side of the river, the side of the Great Light. On the other side of the river, the side of the Great Night, is where we must go. We must cross over the river into the Great Night so that we may gain power to live. We must cross over and cross back. We must replenish our power over others, over our enemies, over the ones who would keep us in pain, in sorrow, in misery. This is the Truth, the one Known Truth, and it will keep us alive, keep us strong, enable us to devour our enemy before he devours us.'

Romeo stood alone in the middle of the room, his eyes closed, his head tilted back. In front of him was an altar surrounded by flickering candles, the only light in the room. On the floor around the circle of light were strewn dozens of crosses, costume jewelry, framed pictures of the saints, dog, cat, cattle and chicken bones, bird feathers, strips of black material, balls of hair, safety pins, saucers filled with milk, silver and gold coins, and pieces of paper with names written on them.

There were approximately sixty people crowded into the room, staring at Romeo or sitting still with their eyes closed, concentrating, listening. Closest to the altar, seated on the floor, were Perdita, Estrellita and Duane. Perdita embraced herself and swayed gently, slowly. Estrellita and Duane held hands level with their waists, their upper arms bound tight to their bodies by clothes-line, their eyelids taped open so that they were unable even to blink.

Adolfo sat to the left and slightly to the rear of Romeo, keeping a steady beat with his hands on both sides of an hourglass drum. Romeo shuddered, his body quivering, then undulating, twisting and turning snakelike, and he began to moan. As he moaned louder and his movements became more spasmodic, others in the room moaned and moved their bodies, gyrating and jerking uncontrollably. The temperature in the already close room became hellish. Sweat poured off the faces of the witnesses, as it did down the forehead and cheeks and bare arms of Romeo Dolorosa, the *nanigo*, the *santero*, the magician, the High Priest of the Goat Without Horns Ceremony.

Romeo opened his eyes and looked around the room. His eyes grew large, then very large, the pupils dilating so that they filled the iris. He began to tremble, to shake more violently now, his eyes bugging out, swelling hideously, seemingly about to burst from his head. His body puffed up like a gigantic mosquito sucking blood from a baby. Adolfo beat harder on the drum, humming and moaning tunelessly, as did most of the witnesses.

The door to the outside opened and two men, wearing white shirts, black pants and black hoods over their heads, entered, carrying the boy, Juan, on a litter, which they placed on the altar. Juan lay perfectly still as the men withdrew into the audience, his eyes closed. He was completely naked and his body had been painted white and covered with sweet-smelling oil and garlic. Romeo bent over the boy and vomited on his chest. Juan's eyes remained closed. Romeo picked up a large knife from the altar and held it over Juan's neck.

'Shango!' Romeo shouted, and suddenly slit the boy's throat.

Blood spurted straight up from the wound like black oil from an uncapped well. It poured out over Romeo, and as he shook himself the blood spattered those closest to him. Juan's legs and arms kicked and flailed and Romeo jumped and danced, groaning and shouting, 'Shango! Shango!' Everyone in the room watched now as Romeo returned to the body and plunged the knife deep into little Juan's chest, sawing and hacking until he had pried loose the boy's heart. Romeo dropped the knife and lifted the bloody, pulsating heart and drank from it, his face, hands, arms and chest shimmering red in the puce light.

Romeo went to the body once more, reached in with both hands, the heart having been discarded on the altar, and pulled out the dripping viscera. He stepped out of the circle, Juan's innards dangling from Romeo's fists, and passed among the observers, many of whom made shrill, shrieking sounds as the possessed *babalao* wiped his soiled hands on their lips and foreheads, smearing them with the sacrificial flesh and blood. Romeo returned to the circle and collapsed. Adolfo ceased his drumming. The people rose and left the room as quickly as possible, pushing together into the night, avoiding each other's eyes.

Only Perdita, Estrellita, Duane and Adolfo remained with Romeo and Juan's mutilated corpse. Perdita and Adolfo both lay down on the floor and fell into a heavy sleep. Estrellita and Duane, their eyes taped open, sat motionlessly, fingers locked, minds frozen. A small calico cat with green eyes came in the open door, walked slowly over to one of the saucers filled with milk, and drank.

'You talk to the girl's parents, too,' Rip asked, 'or just the boy's?'

'I only could get hold of Mrs Satisfy,' said Fed.

'Glory Ann. She says the FBI's already on the job. They got some kind of deal with the Drug Enforcement agents who been after this Romeo Dolorosa for a time now. Apparently the DEA had him set up at Del Rio, but he got away. Now that there's a probable double kidnap across the border, the FBI's buttin' in.'

Rip got up from his desk and walked over to the window. Because of the heat, Calle Brazo was practically deserted at three P.M.

'Don't underrate those boys, Fed. Them and us always has got along good.'

'You gonna follow up on Ramon's tip about a dropoff at Junction?'

'Have to. Figure to camp out on the highway there tonight.'

'Want company?'

'Come if you want, Fed, though I doubt there'll be anything movin' but the usual, wetbacks and coyotes.'

'There is, we'll be on 'em like a king snake on a pegleg rat.'

Rip and Fed headed toward Junction, which was at the extreme southern end of Larry Lee County, fifty miles south of Susie, at nine o'clock that night. Before he'd become a drunk, Ramon Montana had been a lawyer, a successful one, and as such had kept up on most of the significant doings in South Texas. The bottle claimed him now, but Ramon still listened carefully to what people said and how they said it, and he managed to remember about half of what he heard. When he eavesdropped on the Castillo brothers, Eddie and Lou, at the bar in El Loco's, and caught the name Marcello Santos, Ramon, even though he was half in the bag, paid particular attention. One of the Castillos' cousins, Pete Armendariz, was a soldier in the Santos family. Armendariz had recently called the Castillos and talked about having to deliver a truckload of goods down at the Junction highway, after which he intended to drop in on Eddie and Lou. The Castillos were looking forward to Pete's visit.

'With soldiers like Armendariz,' Fed Phillips told Rip, 'ain't no call for Santos to hire a publicity agent.'

Rip laughed. 'Pete ain't exactly the genius in the group,' he said, as they tooled along in the unmarked white Ford Crown Victoria.

At Junction, which was nothing more than a crossroads leading north to McAllen, south to Reynosa, northwest to Laredo, and east to Brownsville and Matamoros, Rip pulled off the road and drove a few hundred yards into the scrub. When he was far enough from the highway not to be spotted, Rip cut the engine and he and Fed got out.

'We'll hike back over and find us some cover,' Rip said. 'Grab that thermos from the back seat. I made fresh coffee. Be interestin' to see if this is gonna turn out to be anything. Just hope it ain't somethin' Ramon overheard in Wild Turkey town. What else you know about this black magic dope-runnin' cult operatin' out of Cándido Aguilar or Zopilote, or wherever it is?'

'Just that the dude runnin' the show, Dolorosa, is supposed to be some kinda supernatural freak can change into a snake or a jaguar. Least that's what the Mexicans say.'

'Nagual.'

'What's that?'

'Nagual's got the body of a jaguar and head of a man. Indians believe only a *brujo* can transform himself like that.'

'Well, whatever he is, he's sure got all the peons between Corpus and Tampico spooked proper. Whole state of Tamaulipas is afraid of this cat and his bunch. Keeps the power over 'em, that's for certain.'

'Religion's about the most powerful force there is, Fed. It's just sex by another name. Think about all the damage been done throughout history in the name of some religion or other. Every blamed war been a so-called holy war. Not much you can do to persuade a person's dead convinced they got God on their side other than get 'em down and make sure they can't get up again.'

'My daddy, Federal Lee Phillips, before he died, used to say, "If God had any mercy in Him, he'd keep me clean."'

'Man had a conscience, Fed. That's somethin' to take refuge in.'

'Just couldn't abide bein' a sinner and not bein' able to do nothin' to prevent it. Finally, he stuck a forty-four in his right ear, the deaf one. You know that Blackhawk I got at the office in the left side bottom desk drawer with the *Hustlers*? That's the weapon he done it with.'

Rip stopped walking.

'This here's prob'ly the best brush for us to hide behind,' he said. 'Got a good view of the crossroads.'

'Rip?'

'Yes, Fed?'

'You reckon there really is a man can change into a jaguar?'

'Doubt it, but I suppose in these times anything's possible.'

'Dolorosa would have to be the devil himself then, Rip, loosed upon the land, not no ordinary human.'

Rip took out his Smith & Wesson .357 revolver, checked to see that it was fully loaded, and replaced it in the holster.

'Like I say, Fed, it wouldn't take more than a little to surprise me. Meantime, all we can do is keep our good eye on the road.'

Tough Boys

Perdita did not like the idea of having to drive all the way to Los Angeles with Estrellita.

'Why can't I drive Duane and you take Estrellita in the truck?' she said.

'What if he overpowers you and steals the Cherokee?' asked Romeo.

'We'll tie him up.'

'Bad idea, *mi amor*. Someone sees the kid, it's trouble. I figure you can handle Estrellita better. She's scared shitless of you, anyway. She won't try anything. And Duane will be under my control. Trust me, *chica*.'

'You know,' said Perdita, as she lit a Marlboro, 'I never like it when you call me "*chica*." Maybe because that guy I used to know I told you about, Bobby Peru, he called me that. He's dead now, of course, and it don't really matter, but I'd just same rather you didn't.'

Romeo closed the back of the Jeep, took out a red and white kerchief from his back pocket and wiped the dust from the tops and toes of his steel-tipped purple and black lizard-skin boots. He replaced the kerchief in his pocket and smiled his movie actor smile at Perdita. Romeo's large white teeth shone in the moonlight. Perdita looked at him. Romeo's teeth were a lot nicer than Bobby's, she thought.

'Didn't realize you were so sensitive, sweetheart,' Romeo said. 'Still got that tough boy in your mind, huh?'

Perdita took a deep drag on her Marlboro, blew out the smoke in a fast, thin pink stream, and flicked the butt off a cactus.

'I ever tell you how he was killed?'

'Not that I remember.'

'He was attemptin' to rob a feed store in West Texas and a patrolman shot him.'

'You saw this happen?'

'No. I heard about it later, on the radio.'

Romeo shrugged his shoulders and dropped his smile.

'Life goes bad that way sometimes,' he said. 'And you move with it from there. You felt something sincere, then, for this Peru.'

'He wasn't no real friendly person. It's not easy to say just what there was between us. I ain't particularly upset he's dead, if that's what you mean.'

'What if I were killed, Perdita, would you mourn?'

Perdita studied Romeo's face hard for a moment, then looked away. She thought about Tony, Juana's husband, and how he'd once tried to force her to suck his cock while Juana was taking a shower. Perdita would have bit it hard if Tony had been able to pry open her mouth but he hadn't. She'd told Juana about it as soon as she came out of the bathroom, and Juana had grabbed a kitchen knife and stuck it into the thigh of Tony's left leg. Perdita could still remember the way Tony's face twisted up with pain and how he staggered out the front door to his Eldorado and drove off to the hospital with the black knife handle sticking up out of his leg. She and Juana had laughed a lot over that one, both then and at later times when one of them would mention it. The thought of Tony hopping to the car made Perdita laugh now. Juana and Tony were dead so there was nobody left but herself to remember what happened and laugh about it.

'Ain't it time we got goin'?' she said.

Bon Voyage

Pete Armendariz was a pill lover. He didn't care what kind of drug or vitamin he ingested, he just enjoyed the act itself, feeling the tablets, big or small, on his tongue, and then the exquisite infusion of water or whisky that washed the round or oblong things down his throat. Tonight Pete had taken six bumblebees, enough speed to keep even a big man like him – six-four, two-seventy – going for up to forty-eight hours, along with his usual evening complement of twelve thousand milligrams of vitamin C; two dozen Stresstabs with zinc, calcium and magnesium; twenty-two Super Hy-Vite time-release multivitamins with twenty-eight nutrients coated with natural alfalfa juice concentrate; and sixteen Giant E-ze with 3-rivers oyster extract to keep his libido bopping. Pete prided himself on his enormous capacity for fucking, fighting and eating. He credited the vitamins with keeping him fit and looking younger than his twenty-nine years.

As he guided the truck closer to Junction, Pete grew more and more excited by the thought of partying with his cousins, Eddie and Lou. It had been no little while since the three of them had done some serious shitkicking together. Pete enjoyed his size, his muscle, his overwhelming appetites. He'd played offensive tackle at Baylor University in Waco for a year, but got kicked off the team for beating up an assistant coach who suggested too strenuously that Pete quit calling the quarterback 'Cunt Lips.' Pete hated quarterbacks, believing they got all the glory while the linemen, such as himself, did all the real work. He played part of another year for the Red Raiders of Texas Tech at Lubbock, but got expelled for sexually assaulting a student nurse who was attempting to prevent Pete from stealing a vial of Darvocet at the university medical center. After college, Pete went to New Orleans, where he tended bar in three or four places until he went to work for the Santos family.

Pete pulled the truck over on the northwest side of the highway, turned off the ignition and jumped down from the cab. Dede Peralta came up right behind the truck in the Lincoln Town Car. Pete walked over to the driver's side of the Lincoln and Dede rolled down his window.

'We're a little early,' said Dede. 'You were really barrelin' that baby.'

Pete grinned, causing his *bandido* mustache to curl up slightly at the ends.

'Got some people to see,' he said. 'Hopin' you could drive me up to Susie, about forty-five minutes from here. I'll get back to NO on my own.'

Dede nodded. 'Don't see why not.'

Romeo and Perdita, accompanied by Duane and Estrellita in the back seat, drove up in the Cherokee and stopped behind the Lincoln. Romeo got out and walked up to Pete.

'I am Romeo Dolorosa.'

'You're right bang on time, Mr Dolorosa,' said Pete. 'Mr Santos appreciates it. Mr Peralta, in the car here, has got your instructions.'

Dede handed a nine-by-twelve-inch manila envelope to Romeo.

'The directions to the delivery location in Los Angeles are very clear,' Dede said. 'If you encounter any difficulties along the way, or once you are in LA, that you are unable to take care of yourself, there is a number to call. Mr San Pedro Sula will meet you at your destination, as you know. Mr Santos says he has great confidence in you, Mr Dolorosa. I know you will justify his faith.'

Romeo saw Rip Ford and Federal Ray Phillips jump out from the dark, guns drawn, just before the sheriff shouted, 'Hands up, *amigos*! Hang 'em on your ears!'

Pete dived to his left and rolled behind the truck before Rip or Fed could squeeze off a shot. Romeo hit the deck and Dede pulled a nine-millimeter Heckler & Koch semi-auto loaded with hot Israeli ammo from his crotch, turned toward the cops and got a bullet between his eyes. The index finger of his right hand locked on the trigger and fired seven rounds through the roof of the Town Car after he was already dead.

Pete crawled under the truck, took out his .45 Browning automatic and blasted away. Romeo heard one of the cops cry out, followed by several more shots, then nothing. He lay on the ground behind the Lincoln, waiting for a voice, a noise. From where he lay, Romeo could not see inside the Cherokee. He shifted his position and looked under the truck, but Pete wasn't there. Romeo waited for thirty seconds before he crawled around the rear of the Town Car. He looked up at the front window of the Cherokee but no faces were visible. He figured that Perdita and the others were on the floor, keeping their mouths shut.

He peered around the end of the car and saw both cops lying perfectly still on the ground. Romeo crawled toward Rip and Fed on his hands and knees, made sure that they were dead, then looked over by the side of the truck for Pete. He was lying on his back, his head toward Romeo, the .45 still in his right hand. Romeo stood up and walked over to him. There was a hole in Pete's chest the size of a silver dollar. He was dead, too. Romeo took the gun out of Pete's hand, then went back over to the cops and took their guns and ammunition belts. He carried the guns and belts to the Cherokee and tapped on the window of the passenger side. Perdita raised her head from the seat.

'Take these and stick them in the lock box,' Romeo said. 'Everyone else is dead. Duane, you come with me in the truck. We'd better get started. It's a long way to go and no tellin' what other fun and games the gods got in store for us.'

Perdita lit a Marlboro. Estrellita was curled up on the back seat, shaking and crying.

'I tell you, Romeo,' said Perdita, 'this bitch of yours don't straighten up, she ain't gonna make it to no California.'

Ghouls

Estrellita watched Perdita smoke. Perdita kept both hands on the steering wheel of the Cherokee and controlled the cigarette with her lips and teeth. She puffed on the Marlboro while it was between her lips and held it in her teeth when she exhaled. Perdita's long, loose black hair rested on the shoulders of her magenta tee shirt. She was wearing black cotton trousers and huaraches. Hidden by her hair were large silver hoop earrings, to each of which was attached a thin strip of red ribbon. Romeo had told her that a piece of red or brown material worn on the body neutralized the power of one's enemies, drained it from them like a grounding wire pulling electricity into the earth.

'How long you been smoking?' Estrellita asked.

Perdita did not respond. She did not really dislike Estrellita; she cared nothing about her.

'I only tried it twice,' said Estrellita. 'The first was in the summer before high school. I was with Thelma Acker at her house when her parents were gone. Her mother had an opened pack of Pall Malls in a kitchen drawer, so we smoked one. Only about half of one, really. I took about three puffs and coughed like crazy every time. Then around a month ago at a Sig Chi party I tried a Sherman. You ever have one of those? They're black. Kind of sweet tastin', too. Didn't care for it, either, though I didn't cough so much as with the Pall Mall.'

Perdita took a final drag on her Marlboro and put it out in the ashtray.

'I know I'm just talkin' about nothin', and that you hate me,' said Estrellita, 'but I'm so scared I don't know what to do. I always talk a lot when I'm nervous. Do you talk a lot when you're nervous? Are you ever nervous? Are you ever gonna talk to me?'

Perdita looked quickly at Estrellita, then back at the road.

'You're gonna murder us, too, eventually,' Estrellita said. 'Isn't that right? Duane isn't very smart, really. I hope you know that. I mean, he's OK so far as pullin' on his pants one leg at a time, but he can't understand you people.'

Perdita grinned slightly. 'Do you?' she asked.

'I think you and Romeo are incredibly deranged individuals with no morals. You're the most evil creatures on the planet. I know you'll kill me soon so I'm sayin' it. My only hope is in the next life, which is what my Aunt Crystal Rae Satisfy always says. Now I know she's been absolutely correct all this time, that it's literal truth. There's too much ugliness on this earth, seein' how it's crawlin' with soulless ghouls.'

'What's a ghoul?' said Perdita.

'What you and Romeo are. The worst kind of evil person. A person who'd violate a corpse.'

Estrellita bit her lower lip but didn't cry.

'Whoever gave you the notion you was God's perfect child?' Perdita said. 'Does Romeo call you Santa Estrellita when you go down on him? He always likes the religious angle. Tell you straight, Miss Satisfy, honey, you're right. It was up to just me, you'd be buried by now out in that desert along with them others. Your blond pussy's what's keepin' you alive, so you'd best make use of it for all it's worth. Girls like you got a kind of sickness, the only way to cure it is to kill it. Always talkin' about love and what's good, that shit, when you're same as me, just no particular piece of trash.'

'You really think that? That we're the same kind of person?'

'Ain't seen no evidence to doubt it.'

'Well, you're plenty wrong, I don't mind tellin' you. God may create people equal, but after that they're on their own.'

Perdita laughed. She shook another Marlboro from the pack on the dash, stuck it between her lips and punched in the lighter. She kept her eyes on the jittery red taillights of the truck.

'A person don't never know who they are till someone knows better tells 'em,' said Perdita. 'A person won't listen might never know, they never stop to hear. Romeo's good at figurin' out people.'

The lighter popped out and Perdita took it and lit her cigarette.

'He's a kind of fake, 'course,' she said, 'but he's got a unlimited way of seein' things. He's got the power to make people believe him.'

'He's horrible,' said Estrellita. 'You're both so horrible I bet God don't even believe it.'

Perdita laughed as she spit out the smoke.

'God don't take everything so serious, *gringa*. You see pretty soon how much He cares about you.'

Lives of the Saints

Romeo turned up the radio. Ernest Tubb was singing 'When a Soldier Knocks and Finds Nobody Home.'

'This is one of my daddy's favorites,' said Duane. 'It's real sad. He used to sing it to us when my brother Herschel Roy and I were small. It and Jimmie Rodgers tunes like "Why Should I Be Lonely" and "Somewhere Down Below the Dixon Line."'

Romeo kept the truck headed west at a safe speed.

'One I always enjoyed was "My Darlin' Clementine,"' Romeo said. 'I seen that old movie, too, where the sheriff, Wyatt Earp, says, "Sure is a hard town for a fella to have a quiet game of poker in," after Doc Holliday runs off a cheater in the Tombstone saloon. The best line, though, is from Walter Brennan, who plays Pa Clanton, father of the meanest boys in the territory. After Earp busts up the sons' tormentin' of a travelin' actor, Brennan comes in and horsewhips 'em, then says, "When you *pull* a gun, kill a man." That's beautiful, Duane.

'Also, when Saint Henry Fonda, who's Wyatt Earp, walks out of the hotel into pourin' rain at three in the mornin' on the night his youngest brother's been killed, he walks alone away from the camera along the plank-covered street, and everything's gray and black streaks, like real life.'

Duane was silent, watching the shadows jump past as the refrigerated truck, carrying two thousand-plus pounds of female detritus, stuck East Texas in its back pocket.

'Man, I remember when I was in Tampa, Florida,' said Romeo, 'seventeen years old, at my grandmother's house, and I saw the movie *Vera Cruz* on television. It changed my life, the way Saint Burt Lancaster looked and talked. He had about 108 giant gleaming teeth, and wore a dusty black outfit and black drawstring hat, a black leather wristband and a silver-studded black gunbelt with a pearl-handled revolver strapped to his right thigh. You ever see that one, Duane?'

Duane shook his head no and stared out the window. The desert at night looked like a tigerskin rug.

'Saint Burt is an outlaw,' Romeo continued, 'operating in Maximilian's Mexico, who hooks up with Saint Gary Cooper, playing a former Confederate colonel from Louisiana who has no desire to live under Yankee rule. Saint Coop's idea is to score enough loot to refinance the Rebel cause. Saint Burt is the greatest gunslinger alive. He can shoot equally well with either hand, and even backhanded! He and Saint Coop and their gang join up with Maximilian rather than Juarez because the Emperor pays better. They agree to help escort a French countess and her carriage to Vera Cruz. The trick, of course, is that a load of gold is hidden in the carriage, and everybody wants it. One of Juarez's generals, Ramirez, pulls a superb stunt when he surrounds Saint Burt and his men on the walls of a town square. Burt rotates his lion's head as dozen after dozen of Ramirez's peasant army appear, and when our Black Saint sees he's trapped, he unleashes his magnificent grin and the world stops, blinded by the glare. The scene resembles a painting by Velásquez.

'Saint Burt's name is Joe Erin; Saint Coop is Ben Train. Joe is slick, crude, flashy, schooled by old Ace Hannah, the man who gunned down Joe's father. And Joe makes a point of telling Ben how and when Joe paid Ace back. Ben Train is elegant, older, gentler. It's sincerely wonderful when Joe says of Ben, "I don't trust him. He likes people; you can never count on a man like that." Joe spills wine on himself when he drinks from a glass. Ben speaks French and charms the countess, much to Joe's dismay. They make a great pair.

'Joe Erin is the kind of man I wanted to be: fierce, daring and dangerous, combined with the elegance of Ben Train. The Great Burt approaches that at the end of *Vera Cruz*, when he and Saint Coop have their showdown. Saint Burt twirls his pistol one last time into his holster before collapsing, grinning more brilliantly than ever as the reluctant but superior shooter Ben Train's bullet takes his life. It is a dramatic ending, Duane, the most perfect ending for a man. It's the path to sainthood.'

'You gonna shoot us, Mr Dolorosa,' said Duane, turning toward Romeo, 'after we get to the West Coast, maybe. Ain't that right?'

Romeo whistled softly, gritted his teeth and grinned.

'We ain't got to that part yet,' he said. 'There's no script, like for a movie. Be best to work things out as we go along, *amigo*, don't you think?'

'I'd appreciate it.'

'Thought you would.'

Communion

'When I was twelve years old,' said Estrellita, 'my mama and I and my friend Daisy Samples and her cousin Cutie Lewis were sitting on our front porch one summer evenin' talkin', when here come the preacher and his wife, and couple or three children and a pair or more other poor relations, to find out why it was our family hadn't been to church lately.

'"Evenin', Mrs Satisfy," the preacher said. "Evenin', Estelle. Evenin' all of you." We're Baptists, sort of. What I mean by that is none of us is really much on churchgoin' any more. When I was real small we went more, maybe two or three times a month. But it was around the time I'm talkin' about, I guess, that we began to really slack off.

'Anyway, the preacher's talkin' about how terrible wet the air is, and how that brings out the mosquitoes, and so on, and his dumb kids are scratchin' and kickin' at each other, fightin', bored out of their skulls, the mother's shushin' 'em, and the couple of dumb souls are startin' to wander off in different directions. So the preacher asks mama why we ain't been around in church lately, and she tells him things has been shaky with her and Ernest Tubb, but we'll be back in by and by, the next Sunday, prob'ly.

'Then he asks Daisy Samples if she'd be interested in comin' on Sunday, too, and Daisy says, "Not me, preacher, I'm a Catholic." Well, this takes the preacher back, 'cause you know how bad the Baptists hate the Catholics. He keeps up his smile, though, and turns to Daisy's cousin, Cutie, but before he can ask her, my mama, Glory Ann, says, "Don't think you'll be wantin' her, either, seein' how Cutie's half a Catholic and half a Jew."

'Whew! Hearin' that word, *Jew*, just stunned the man, and he begun herdin' his people back to the car, tippin' his beat-up gray slouch hat with the sweat stripe around the middle, and tellin' mama and me he'd see us in church. I don't recall whether we went that week or not.'

Perdita kept her eyes on the road.

'We were Catholics,' she said.

'Did you go to church a lot?'

'When I was young, I did. Didn't impress me much, though, not like it did my sister, Juana. She was sold on it for a bit, until our neighbor, Cruz Fierro, told her about how the nuns ate their own babies.'

Estrellita looked at Perdita, then out the passenger side window. Blue shark's teeth nibbled at the black curtain.

'What do you mean, ate their babies?'

'To get rid of the evidence, so nobody'd find 'em. Better than buryin' bodies could be dug up. Cruz was a hustler up in Houston, and a junkie, but he wasn't a liar. The dope killed him. He made it with a priest, who told him that a nun who had a baby was made to eat it herself, as a punishment. That turned Juana off from wantin' to be a bride of God. She married that fucker Tony instead.'

Perdita laughed. 'Juana woulda done better,' she said, 'even if she'd had to eat her own kid. Might be she'd still be alive.'

Woody Dumas, special agent in charge of the United States Drug Enforcement Administration's regional office in Dallas, leaned back in his chair and put his feet up on his desk. He tore open a jumbo bag of salted peanuts and cracked and ate them as he spoke.

'I'm hearin' you, Doyle, loud and clear,' Woody said into the telephone cradled between his left cheek and shoulder, 'no need to shout. Don't take no whiz kid to figure out Santos is involved at the top of the deck, either. This the first you FBI geniuses heard of him? OK, OK, Mr Cathcart, sir! Soon as I got a bead on these tree squirrels, you'll know about it. My guess is they got some *maquila* around El Paso, but could be they're movin' the goods all the way to the West Coast. I got my best bird dogs on hunt, so don't take a header. You bet, Doyle, good buddy. *Adiós* for now, huh?'

Woody hung up, cracked open another peanut and popped it into his mouth. He'd turned fifty the day before but looked ten years younger. He still had a full head of thick, sandy brown hair and a mostly unwrinkled face. Woody Dumas had never married and never been tempted to. At six-two and one-eighty-five, he moved at a leisurely pace, took a multivitamin pill daily with his orange juice, didn't eat sweets or drink coffee, worked out three times a week on a LifeCycle and with weights at the Downtown Health Club, and got at least six hours of sleep each night. His favorite reading material was the sports section of the newspaper. Woody did not believe in cluttering up his mind with a lot of unnecessary information. Life was complicated enough, he felt, without mixing in a bunch of half-baked ideas.

Woody knew that Crazy Eyes Santos was behind the skin business, just as he was behind virtually every other major illegal enterprise across the South and Southwest. The Mexicans had tied him to most of the cocaine and marijuana being smuggled across the border, and Doyle Cathcart, the special agent in charge of the Federal Bureau of Investigation office in Houston, was certain that Santos was using his dope network to transport experimental cosmetic materials. There was some ugly shit going on down around the border, too, that Woody had been hearing about, all kinds of so-called religious garbage, including animal and even human sacrifice.

At precisely four-thirty P.M., Woody Dumas swung his maroon and white Tony Lama boots to the floor, tossed the bag of peanuts on the desk and stood up. He brushed himself off, picked his white Stetson from the hatrack and placed it firmly on his head. There was more sickness in the world today, Woody believed, than at any time in history. Walking out of the Federal Building he thought of an incident he'd read about in the *Morning News*, something that had taken place in San Francisco shortly after the recent earthquake there. A man named DeSota Barker had been directing traffic at a busy intersection after the city-wide power failure knocked out the stoplights, and an impatient, probably cracked-out motorist had shot and killed him. Barker was subsequently listed among the victims of the earthquake.

'The more things there are to figure,' Woody thought, 'the more things there are get figured wrong.'

He climbed behind the wheel of his brown 1978 Malibu Classic and cranked it up. Woody sat in the car, letting the engine idle, thinking about Salty Dog, the Airedale he'd had when he was a boy. When Woody was fourteen and the dog was four, Salty had bitten two old ladies – one while she was watering her lawn, the other as she was walking up the steps to her house – within a week. He'd never bitten anyone before that, but the county took Salty away and put him to sleep. Woody didn't understand why he thought about Salty Dog almost every day at this time. It had been thirty-six years since they'd gassed Salty, Woody realized, and the world just hadn't been right since.

The Big Day

'Didn't you tell me you used to live out here?' Romeo asked Perdita.

They were at the Rim City Truck-o-Rama, fueling up.

It was not quite six o'clock of a new day. Perdita looked around. A sharp wind came up and blew sand into her face. She put on her sunglasses.

'Not too far,' Perdita said.

She pulled a Marlboro out of the pack she'd stuck in the front of her Wranglers and put it between her lips but did not try to light it. Perdita walked over to where a dozen Macks and Peterbilts dozed, night sweat sparkling on their metallic hides. She kicked at a wad of red mud caked on one of the giant tires.

'How you doin'?'

Perdita turned around. It was Duane. She still had the unlit cigarette in her mouth, so Duane took a book of matches from his pocket and fired it. He watched Perdita's straight black hair fly back from her Chiricahua cheekbones like a quarter horse's tail in deep stretch at Ruidoso Downs. The weak sun brushed red streaks on it.

'We gonna drive straight through, you think,' Duane asked, 'or what?'

'Romeo'll likely want to sleep during the day and drive at night. You figure you and Little Miss Poison maybe could slip out on us?'

Duane half-laughed. 'I don't guess,' he said.

Perdita leaned back against the tire she'd kicked.

'You ever think that someone might be watchin' us?' she asked.

'Who someone?'

Perdita took a hard drag on her Marlboro, then flicked it away.

'I mean some kind of super intelligent bein'. Somethin' invisible, like a ghost. Someone who knows everything's goin' on.'

'Guess it's possible. Sounds like you're talkin' about God, though.'

Perdita shook her head. 'This ain't no god.'

'Why can't we see him then?'

'He'll step in on his own sweet time. When the big day comes, and it's comin' quick.'

'What'll happen on the big day?'

'Snakes and spiders, rainin' on the people.'

'Heard that after the hurricane in South Carolina last month, snakes was everywhere. Moccasins, copperheads, all kinds, blown out of the swamps.'

'This'll be worse. He knows what we're doin', all of us. There ain't nobody innocent, not you, not me, not Estrellita.'

'Or Romeo.'

Perdita nodded. 'Sky'll fall on him, too. Maybe especially on him.'

The sun stood up and chopped the chill in two.

'Hey, you two lovebirds!' Romeo shouted from where he was pumping gas. 'Let's go inside the cafe here and get some breakfast.'

The four of them sat in a booth. Bill Monroe was singing 'A Fallen Star' on the jukebox. After they'd ordered, Romeo went over to the cashier's stand, bought a *San Antonio Light*, came back and sat down.

'Now here's a good one,' he announced, 'about a guy named Bubba Ray Billy, a con in Angola, Louisiana, who got fried yesterday. Seems this Billy, who was twenty-six, raped and murdered by stabbing seventeen times an eighteen-year-old girl named Lucy Fay Feydaux. Bubba Ray had picked up Lucy Fay, it says, in his 1954 blue and white Oldsmobile Holiday on a country road outside Opelousas one night four years ago. "He must of took her against her will," said the girl's mother, Irma. Mr Archie Bob Feydaux, Lucy Fay's father, attended the execution and told reporters that he and his wife supported the death penalty and had been waiting four years for Billy to die.'

Their food had begun to arrive while Romeo was reading, and he gulped down his orange juice and half a cup of coffee before continuing to paraphrase and quote from the paper. Perdita kept her dark glasses on and smoked her way through the meal while Duane and Estrellita kept their heads down as they ate their eggs, toast, sausages and grits.

'So the good old boys over to Angola strapped Bubba Ray Billy into Gruesome Gertie,' Romeo said, 'the big oak electric chair, and ended Archie Bob and Irma Feydaux's vigil. Billy was one mean cat, according to this. He'd had a Grim Reaper tattooed on his chest while in the Death House and confessed to at least two other killings in addition to the kidnapping and attempted murder of a Poplarville, Louisiana, teenager and the rape of the boy's girlfriend.

'"I don't run from nothing," Billy said. "People say I'm an animal, but they wouldn't say it to my face. I wouldn't say I'm an animal," he told reporters, "but I am a cold person." Boy was a regular case, wouldn't you say, Perdita, honey? Get this: his daddy, Guinn "Boss" Billy, spent twenty-eight of his fifty-five years in the slam for cattle theft, aggravated battery and manslaughter. When queried by the press as to his reaction to Bubba Ray's impending execution, Boss Billy just told them that he would sleep through it and said his son deserved to die.'

Romeo whistled long and softly through his teeth.

'Man, the boy's daddy's an even harder case. This last part's the best. Bubba Ray apparently didn't talk much during the big day. He ate a last supper of fried oysters and shrimp, even though, as he said, he didn't feel much like eating. When a reporter commented to him that he'd nevertheless cleaned his plate, Billy smiled a little and said, "I guess some old habits is just tough to break."'

Romeo put down the newspaper, stabbed a pat of butter with his knife and stuck it in his bowl of oatmeal, poured half a glass of milk over it, and signaled for the waitress, who was an elderly, lame Mexican woman with one half-shut eye.

'Señora,' he said, when she limped over, 'I sure would appreciate it if you could scare up some molasses for me to sweeten up this cereal. Oatmeal just don't taste the same without it.'

A Visit to Sparky & Buddy's

'You want the usual, Mr Dumas?'

'Maybe a little extra ice, Sherry Louise, if you don't mind. It's a warm one.'

Woody loosened his tie and arched his back. He didn't like sitting on stools but tonight, for some reason, he felt unusually tired. Ordinarily, he stood at the bar. It was a slow evening at Sparky & Buddy's; there were only two other customers in the place.

'There you go, Mr Dumas, cranberry juice and soda with a slice of orange, two maraschino cherries and extra ice, in a chimney.'

'Sherry Louise, you take good care of me and I want you to know that I appreciate it.'

Woody slid a five dollar bill to her across the black mahogany.

'This is yours,' he said.

'It's my pleasure, Mr Dumas. Always is.'

Woody watched Sherry Louise walk back to the other end of the bar. She undulated, like a giraffe. She must be a half-inch or so over six feet tall, Woody figured, in the green and white New Balance running shoes she wore while she was on duty. Her bright red hair was piled up on her head, adding a good three or four inches of height. Tall and *mucho* skinny, too skinny for his taste, Woody decided. Sherry Louise looked like a section of two-inch pipe stood on end with a bird's nest set on top. She was extra sweet, though, and Sparky said she was the most dependable and honest bartender they'd ever had. Her husband, Eddie Dean Zernial, a former stock car driver, was a carpet layer. Sherry Louise was always going on about how messed up Eddie Dean's back and knees were, both from collisions and rug tacking, but one night she'd told Woody that didn't interfere with their sex life any, since she preferred riding high to lying low. Woody had a difficult time imagining what it would be like to make love to

Sherry Louise. It was better that way, he thought; one less thing to have to think about.

A short, stout man of about forty came in and sat down two stools to Woody's left. He was perspiring heavily and used a bar napkin to wipe the sweat from his mostly bald head. Sherry Louise smiled at Woody as she passed him.

'What can I do you for, handsome?' she asked the man.

He held up his right hand and horizontally extended three fingers.

'Wild Turkey,' the man said, 'straight. Water chaser, with plenty of ice.'

'Appears all you gentlemen need coolin' down this evenin',' said Sherry Louise. 'Ain't all that hot, I don't think.'

She poured the whisky into a double shot glass, filled another with ice and tap water and set them both in front of the customer. He put his money on the bar, Sherry Louise took it, walked to the cash register, made change and brought it back.

'Just shout, you need me,' she told him, and smiled again at Woody. 'You all right for now, Mr Dumas?'

Woody smiled at her. 'Just fine, Sherry Louise.'

'Sons of bitches ain't never gonna find her,' said the short, bald man.

Woody turned toward him.

'Come again?'

'Go over that border don't expect no favors, what I always say.'

'Woody Dumas,' said Woody, offering his right hand to the man.

'Ernest Tubb Satisfy,' he said, giving Woody's hand a quick, wet shake, after which Ernest Tubb picked up the shot glass and sipped noisily.

'What border you mean?' Woody asked.

'Messican, 'course. Chink counterfeiters makin' Rolexes, computer innards, that shit, government'll go after like cockstarved banshees. Let it be some poor little Texas gal gets grabbed off the street and they can't figure their asshole wipes north or south. Yesterday on the Blaupunkt in my Mark IV, I heard about G-men bustin' a Hong Kong ring of fake soy sauce manufacturers. Seized more than one hundred thousand bottles of bogus soy along with the perpetrators. Economics is what it is, pure smilin' simple. That's what I say.'

Ernest Tubb swallowed the rest of his three fingers, gave it a fast chase and cracked an ice cube with his back teeth.

'Goin' after 'em myself,' he said. 'Glory Ann, she thinks I'll get myself killed, but a man's gotta do what he feels deepest in his heart is the right thing. That's what I say. So I'm goin' after Estelle. She's my baby.'

Ernest Tubb hopped down from his stool.

'Good talkin' to ya,' he said to Woody, and walked out.

Sherry Louise came over.

'What was Elmer Fudd there so fired up about?' she asked.

'Man's on a mission of some kind,' said Woody. 'No doubt about it.'

'Ain't much left in this lonesome world got no doubt in it,' Sherry Louise said.

Woody laughed. 'No real comfort in knowin' that, either, I suppose.'

Sherry Louise cleared away Ernest Tubb Satisfy's glasses and wiped the bar clean.

'Seems like sometimes bein' even a little intelligent just don't pay, Mr Dumas. You know what I mean?'

Critics

'Thought it'd be a good idea to see a movie,' said Romeo. 'Might relax everybody a little bit.'

Romeo, Perdita, Duane and Estrellita were in a room at the Orbit Motel in Buck's Bend, New Mexico, halfway between El Paso and Las Cruces. It was four o'clock in the afternoon; they'd slept eight hours.

'We can get back on the highway right after it's over, when it's dark. Noticed on the way into town one of them multi-theater complexes out at the shopping center. What kind of pictures you like, Estrellita, honey?'

Estrellita sneezed and coughed.

'You catchin' cold?' asked Romeo.

'I'm OK,' said Estrellita. 'I don't care much what show we see.'

'What about you, Duane?'

'Don't care.'

'Hey, c'mon everybody! Cheer up!' said Romeo. 'After all, I'm buyin'.'

Perdita did not comment.

Romeo herded everyone into the Cherokee, leaving the truck parked under the Orbit sign, which was an orange neon planet with a purple spaceship, connected on one side by a metal spoke. Several yellow-white stars twinkled on and off around the planet, and a few that didn't work buzzed and hissed.

At the movie complex, Romeo said, 'This *Shocker* sounds like fun. Accordin' to the poster here, a mass murderer gets sentenced to the electric chair, only instead of it killin' him, he feeds on the juice and becomes crazier and more powerful. Let's go.'

Romeo bought the tickets and they went inside. The movie turned out to be even more bizarre than the advertising promised. An insane, sadistic killer, who'd worked as a television repairman and with other electronic devices, is scheduled to die, and his last request in the prison is for a TV set. He hooks his hands up to the television tubes with jumper cables and transfuses himself with electrical current. The guards rush in and disconnect him, and in the ensuing struggle he practically bites off one's lower lip and breaks another's fingers. When they finally give him the big jolt, the chair and the entire penitentiary power system shorts out, and the killer's electrified self, in the form of phantom particles, escapes and wreaks havoc all over again. The film moves back and forth between dreams and reality, and the monster manages to plug himself into a satellite and transmit his ens through television all across the country. He runs rampant among cable and network landscapes until he's programmed into oblivion by the hero, who's been chasing him over the airwaves.

'Man, I'll bet that con in Louisiana,' Romeo said when they were all back outside after the movie, 'Bubba Somethin'', who got singed the other day, woulda asked for a TV set, too, instead of shrimp and oysters, if he'd seen this picture first.'

'It was kinda interestin',' said Duane.

'I enjoyed the hell out of it,' said Romeo. 'Just shows how capital punishment don't really make much of a difference, after all. What'd you girls think?'

'It was disgusting,' Estrellita said. 'These kinds of movies are for morons.'

'Hear that, Duane?' laughed Romeo. 'Your sweetheart here's callin' you a moron.'

'Least he's got company,' said Perdita, lighting up a Marlboro.

'Well, Duane, *amigo*, there you go,' Romeo said. 'Everyone's a critic. No wonder now, is it, why the world's in such a mess. Can't nobody agree on nothin'.'

The Choice

Marcello Santos was unhappy. Dede Peralta had been a long-time associate of his, a friend in a business where few men could truly consider themselves friends. Dede was dead, as was his soldier Pete Armendariz, and Crazy Eyes was upset. He had called a meeting to be held in the farmhouse of his six thousand acre property west of New Orleans. Set in the middle of a swamp, with only one heavily guarded road leading in and out, it was the only place Santos felt totally safe. He had named this haven '*Il Giardino d'Infanzia*,' the nursery. It was as The Nursery that Santos and others, including federal and local police agencies, referred to it in conversation. A small handpainted sign hanging over the entrance to the house read, 'Three can keep a secret if two are dead.'

Present at the meeting, called for eight o'clock on a Tuesday night, were Santos; Alfonse 'Tiger Johnny' Ragusa, the crime boss of Houston and El Paso; Beniamino 'Jimmie Hunchback' Calabrese, a capo in the Gambino family, from New York; Nicky 'Bigfoot' DeAngelis, the Alabama and West Florida drug king; Reggie San Pedro Sula, who stood by Marcello; and the bodyguards for each of the others: 'Papaya Phil' Romo, with Ragusa; Provino 'The Fist' Momo, with Calabrese; and Vincent 'Pit Bull' Deserio, with DeAngelis.

The air conditioning was fighting a losing battle against the ninety-five-degree heat and ninety-nine-percent humidity of the Southern Louisiana night. Santos took off his jacket and mopped his forehead with a black silk handkerchief.

'Thank you, gentlemen,' he said, 'for coming to The Nursery. You all know how this tragedy of Dede has hit me so hard. I have been in mourning since the news reached me. The reason for calling you together is that we have a problem, a most serious problem, that, if we are going to be able to continue what has been so far a profitable participation in the cosmetics trade, we must solve.

'The problem is this Dumas, who is, of course, the special agent of the Drug Enforcement Agency in Dallas. Our friend from Dallas, Joseph Poca, whom you all know as "Joe Polkadots," is, unfortunately, at the present time in prison. Therefore, we are empowered, with the permission of Joe Polkadots, that I have very recently obtained, to act on our own behalf concerning special agent Dumas. I call for suggestions.'

'Marcello,' said Tiger Johnny, 'I'll be happy to take care of this creep. He is, after all, in Texas, which is my state. I can arrange for a pipe bomb to be placed in the man's car, and it will be done. Allow me this privilege.'

'A thought,' said Jimmie Hunchback. 'It might be wiser to have an outside representative handle the job. Why not I leave The Fist here go up to Dallas to take care of it himself? Killing a federal agent is a thing the government won't forget, but in this case I don't think they'd suspect someone from my part of the country.'

'Nicky Bigfoot,' said Santos, 'what do you feel is the correct thing?'

At seventy-nine, Nicky DeAngelis was the oldest of the group. He had ruled the Florida Gulf Coast area for forty years, and Marcello sincerely respected his opinion. Like Santos, Nicky Bigfoot, who earned his nickname because he'd made a large and lasting impression in the course of his career, wore dark glasses most of the time. Unlike Santos, who wore them to cover up his strange eyes, Nicky used them so that he could catnap without anyone knowing he was dozing off. His bodyguard, Pit Bull Deserio, was fiercely protective of his boss, and listened closely to everything that was said in his presence in case Nicky needed him to whisper into his ear any information the old man had missed. Deserio did this now, and it took several moments before Nicky responded to Santos's question.

'I go with Jimmie the Hunch,' said Bigfoot. 'You understand that's how come he's called Jimmie Hunchback. Not because he's got a crippled back, which, as you can see, he don't. If he says his man will do the job right, we should honor his judgment. With all respect to you, Johnny Ragusa, it should be a hitter from someplace out of Texas.'

Santos held up his left hand, the one minus a thumb.

'It's settled, then,' he said. 'Jimmie's man, Provino Momo, will take care of the agent Dumas. Now we can relax and play some serious pinochle! Reggie, give Signore DeAngelis another cup espresso so he can't say he's asleep when I beat him with the cards. Everyone, have more wine, whisky, whatever you want. There is plenty food, also, spaghetti and oysters. You know we like to eat in Louisiana!'

Santos held up a glass filled with wine in his right hand.

'To you, *Il Pugno*, our blessing. And to us all, *salute!*'

Rubout

'Thanks, especially, for sending up the files on Dolorosa and Durango, Doyle. They're quite a pair.'

Woody Dumas had been reading the FBI reports on the skin-business smugglers that Doyle Cathcart had faxed to him overnight, and Doyle had just telephoned to make sure the information had arrived.

'Didn't recall who she was right away,' Woody said, 'but that name, Perdita Durango, was stuck in my head from someplace.'

'She was hooked up with that feed store holdup awhile back in Iraaq,' said Doyle. 'Remember? One of the stickup men got his head blown off and the other one was captured and sent to Huntsville. The Durango gal was the getaway driver, and danged if she didn't get clean away.'

'So now you figure she's mixed up with this barefootin' dope dealer.'

'Right. He's also some kind of *santería* priest. They apparently murdered a boy in a ceremony, and the Mexicans want 'em.'

'Well, I'm about to saddle up, buddy, and get on the trail. Word is the target is in Los Angeles, so I'm headin' west.'

'Just watch your tail, fella. They shoot horses, don't they? They'll sure as shit shoot you, too.'

Woody laughed. ''Preciate your concern, son. You take care, too, now. Hear?' he said, and hung up.

Jimmie Hunchback's best boy, Provino Momo, sat in a rented dark gray Ford Thunderbird across the street from the Federal Building. The Fist was an expert at sitting and waiting. As a child, he'd had tuberculosis and had to spend nearly two years resting. During those two years, from the age of eleven until he was thirteen, The Fist mostly slept and read comic books. An only son, he was not allowed to play at all with other children during his illness, and was kept on a strict low-fat, salt-free diet. He didn't realize how angry he had become during this hiatus until five years later when, during a disagreement in a poolhall in the Red Hook section of Brooklyn, the now fully-grown Provino Momo beat a forty-year-old man to death with his hands. It was from this incident that his nickname derived. Word got around about this big, tough, quiet kid with the grip of steel – he was six-four, two-fifty at eighteen – and The Fist went to work as a soldier for the Gambinos, New York's largest organized crime family. Eventually, he earned the confidence of Jimmie Hunchback, and became the capo's right-hand man.

Now, as The Fist sat in the rented T-bird, watching for the Drug Enforcement agent whose photograph he had next to him on the front seat, he thought about the various men and women he had personally whacked on behalf of the business. Usually, The Fist avoided this kind of rumination, but for some reason, perhaps because he would turn forty years old tomorrow, the same age as his first victim had been, he allowed himself to review this side of his life. Altogether, The Fist figured, he had murdered at least twenty people, most of them without any weapons other than his own hands. That wasn't so many, he thought, not in twenty-two years. He didn't know whether to be pleased or not by this, but his reverie ended a moment later, as soon as he spotted Woody Dumas walking out of the building.

Woody's Malibu was parked directly across from The Fist's T-bird. The agent unlocked his car, got in, started it up and drove away. Didn't even check for a bomb, The Fist thought, as he followed him, wondering why anyone who made a halfway decent living would drive such a crummy-looking car. Maybe these federal guys didn't get paid so well. In any case, he figured, Dumas could drive a better short than this turd-colored piece of junk. It looked too much like a cop car to even be a cop car. The Fist owned an identical pair of white '88 Cadillac Sedan de Villes. He drove them on alternate days, and when one of them was in the repair shop he always had the twin to use. Even though it was too small for a man his size, he didn't mind driving this T-bird. It had pretty good pickup and held the road OK. He wouldn't hesitate to rent another one.

Woody drove slowly through the downtown traffic headed toward his athletic club, which was in the newly gentrified warehouse district. He wanted to get in a good workout before the trip to LA. After parking his car in the alley behind the club, Woody opened the trunk to get his gear. As he bent over to take out his gym bag, the trunk lid came down hard on his back, causing his legs to collapse. Woody fell to the ground. All he could see were two large, brightly polished brown Cordovans. Woody reached his right hand down to his left ankle and pulled from its holster his Charter Arms Bulldog Pug .44 long snub-nose revolver. He felt himself being lifted and squeezed at the same time. Suddenly, he found it very difficult to breathe and realized he was being crushed to death by an enormously powerful person. Woody brought his backup gun as close to his own head as he could and just as he was about to lose consciousness glimpsed the face of his attacker. He squeezed the trigger, hoping the business end was pointed in the right direction.

The Fist fell backward, his gigantic fingers still gripping the agent's arms, so that when Woody again opened his eyes he saw that he was lying on top of a huge man without a nose. The gun had discharged point blank into The Fist's face and the Glazer safety slug had ripped apart his nostrils, leaving an ugly, large red hole above his upper lip and between his two bloodshot eyes, both of which were wide open and staring up emptily at Woody.

A vision of Salty Dog came immediately to Woody's mind, and he closed his eyes and rolled off The Fist on to his back. Salty was chasing an old woman who was wearing a black raincoat, the tail of which the bounding Airedale held tightly in his teeth.

'Get her, Salty,' Woody said. 'Get her, boy!'

Out of the Past

Mona came up for air and Santos barked at her, 'No, no, *cara mia*, don't stop! I'm almost there!'

'I need a break, Marcello, please. My mouth gets tired, and besides, look, it's *fiacco*.'

Santos groaned heavily.

'Everything is difficult these days. Life is *una pioggia continua*.'

Mona got up off her knees and went over to the bar, put a teaspoonful of sugar in a glass, half-filled it with Bombay Sapphire, stirred it with a red swizzle stick that had the words RIZZO'S SOCIAL CLUB • NEW ORLEANS lettered on it in gold, and took a healthy swallow.

'Relax, Marcello,' she said. 'I'm gonna take a bath.'

Crazy Eyes Santos watched his mistress of ten years, Mona Costatroppo, walk out of the room. He listened to the water run into the bathtub. Mona was thirty-one years old, still beautiful, Santos thought, but no longer slim-figured. When he'd first seen her, working as a teller in Grimaldi's bank in Gretna, she looked like Claudia Cardinale, only skinnier. The big dark-brown eyes, long mouth with thick red lips, perfect uptilted breasts. Mona ate too many syrup-filled chocolates now, and drank too much of that fancy gin. Two more years of this, Santos figured, and she'd look exactly like his wife, Lina. At least Lina had provided him with four children.

'Marcello,' Mona called from the bathroom. 'Be a *costata di agnello* and bring me another drink, would you?'

Santos stood, stuffed his penis inside his pants, and zipped them up. He walked out of the apartment and closed the door softly behind him.

'Marcello!' Mona shouted. 'Marcello, are you coming? And don't forget the sugar!'

Detour

A few miles east of Tucson, Romeo turned south off the interstate. He checked his sideview to make sure that Perdita had made the unexpected turnoff in the twilight.

'One thing about our little Apache princess there, Duane boy,' Romeo said, 'she can handle a vehicle good as any man, better than most.'

'Why we takin' this two-lane all of a sudden?'

'There's an *hombre* I'd like to see in Nogales, on the Mexico side, long as we're so close by. Man owes me. Name's Amaury "Big Chief" Catalina. Calls himself Big Chief because he claims he's a direct descendant of some Aztec king. Hell, we're all descendants of one kind of king or other. Runs a restaurant called La Florida. Pretty sure he'll be there, unless he's dead, which he should be. Man shouldn't get used to owin', Duane. It's unhealthy.'

In the Cherokee, Perdita pulled on the lights.

'What's our hero up to now?' she asked herself, following the large white refrigeration truck down Arizona State Highway 82.

'What did you say?' said Estrellita, who was about half awake.

Perdita looked quickly at her, then fastened her eyes back on the narrow, darkening road. She hated the girl's bright blond hair.

'Sonoita? Patagonia? Where are we?' Estrellita asked, reading a distance sign.

Perdita punched in the dash lighter, put a cigarette between her teeth, and as soon as the lighter popped back pulled it out and lit up.

'You sure smoke a hell of a lot,' Estrellita said.

'Won't be botherin' you too much longer, I got anything to say about it. Don't you worry.'

They rode in silence until Romeo rolled through the crossroads that was Sonoita and headed for Patagonia. Perdita had no choice but to follow the white truck.

'Must be he's goin' to see someone owes him money,' she said. 'Just another detour on our way to nowhere.'

At Patagonia, a one-street town about twenty miles north of the border, Romeo pulled the truck over and stopped. Perdita slid the Cherokee to a halt right behind him. Romeo hopped down and came over to Perdita's window, which she lowered all the way.

'Bet you're wonderin' what I'm up to, huh, ladies? Well, there's a kind of spooky gentleman in Nogales, on the Mex side, I mean to pay a quick call on, see if I can shake some of what he owes me out of his jeans. We'll be on our way to LA again in no time. Perdita, sweet thing, in Nogales I'll park this rig on the US side, in the Safeway foodstore lot. We'll leave both vehicles there and walk across the border. I think Estrellita, here, and our good buddy Duane will behave proper, don't you? Now I'm just gonna make a phone call from the booth over there next to the old railway depot. Shouldn't take long.'

In the telephone booth Romeo opened the manila envelope Dede Peralta had given him. He found the sheet of paper he was looking for and held it up to read the number as he dialed. Romeo dropped in the necessary coins, and after the third ring someone answered.

A man's voice said, very softly, 'Bayou Enterprises.'

'This is Romeo Dolorosa. I'd like to speak with Mr Santos, please.'

'Mr Santos is out of town. What's this about?'

'I just wanted to tell him that I'll be a little late to the party. I'm having car trouble, but it's being fixed. Can you please convey this information to Mr Santos when you speak to him?'

'Sure, he keeps in touch. That it?'

'Yes, that's all. Tell him I'll be there as soon as I can.'

'I'm sure you will,' the man said, and hung up.

Romeo hung up on his end and walked back over to Perdita. He smiled at her and leaned forward with one hand on either side of the door.

'Santos isn't a man to fuck with, Romeo,' she said. 'I hope you're not fucking with him.'

'I can handle it, Perdita, darlin'. You know me.'

Her eyebrows twitched, the snakes coiling, but Perdita said nothing as she watched Romeo walk to the truck and climb back in.

'Bet you wish sometimes you didn't,' said Estrellita.

Perdita started up the Cherokee and followed along. A half hour later she parked behind Romeo in the Safeway lot in Nogales. All of them got out.

'You kids do what I say and you'll be all right,' Romeo told Duane and Estrellita. 'If either of you say anything to the customs, I'll shoot you both on the spot, and the customs officer, too. OK, *vámonos*.'

The four of them filed through the turnstile into Mexico. Romeo led them past rows of beggars and through a maze of hustlers and shills, down a comparatively deserted sidestreet and into a courtyard. A white neon sign that said BILLARES blinked and sputtered over one of two doors. Over the other was a dull yellow globe with *LA FLORIDA* painted on it in black script.

'My memory's not so bad,' laughed Romeo. 'It's been four or five years since I've been here. Come on, let's go in.'

There was a long bar to the right of the entrance, and perhaps a dozen tables to the left in front of a small stage. Several men sat at the bar; none of them were well-dressed. Only two of the tables were occupied. A man in a shabby black tuxedo with a red cummerbund came up to Romeo and asked if the four of them were there for dinner.

'Possibly,' said Romeo. 'We'll see.'

The host smiled and showed them to a table.

'*Señor Catalina está aquí?*' asked Romeo, as they were seated.

'He will arrive in perhaps ten minutes,' said the host, who gave each of them a menu. 'Are you a friend of his?'

'Oh yes,' said Romeo, 'a very old one.'

'I will tell him you are here when he comes in. What is your name?'

'Dolorosa. Just say Dolorosa.'

The host kept his smile and said, 'As you wish. Your waiter will be with you in a moment.'

When the waiter came, Romeo ordered margaritas all around. He'd drunk half of his when he saw Amaury Catalina approaching, weaving sharklike through the other tables. The Big Chief was not smiling.

'Romeo, *amigo! Qué tal?* What a marvelous surprise to see you!' Catalina exclaimed, smiling now with every part of his round brown face except the eyes, which were hard and dull, motionless black pellets.

Romeo rose and embraced him.

'I thought it might be,' Romeo said, also smiling a smile without mirth.

Big Chief Catalina was topheavy, carrying well over two hundred pounds on his medium-large five-foot-ten-inch frame. With his caterpillar mustache and thinning black hair greased straight back on his wide, flat head, Catalina looked ten years older than his thirty-four.

'Say, Chief, why don't we go someplace and talk?'

'Of course, of course. We can use my office.'

'Be back shortly, Perdita,' said Romeo. 'You keep an eye on the kids. Make sure they eat their vegetables.'

Catalina signaled to the waiter, who came over immediately.

'See that these people have anything they want,' said the Big Chief, 'without charge.'

Catalina's office was an eight-by-eight windowless box, with a desk, two chairs, and a filing cabinet. On the wall to one side of the desk was a postcard photo of Pancho Villa on his horse in front of his army in 1914. Catalina took a bottle of Gusano Rojo mezcal and two glasses from a drawer and put them on top of the desk, then poured double doses for Romeo and himself.

'Before you ask me about the money, *amigo*, we have a drink, yes? This is good mezcal, from Oaxaca.'

'*Cómo no?*'

'To your health!'

They swallowed the shots of mezcal and set the glasses back on the desk.

'Now, Señor Pain, you can ask me about the money.'

'Do you have it?'

'No. I have money, but not for you, unfortunately.'

'Do you mean that you do not have it for me now, or that you will never have it for me?'

Catalina laughed abruptly but did not smile.

'This is a choice you are welcome to make. Choose the answer that makes you most comfortable.'

'May I have another drink?'

'Of course, help yourself.'

Romeo stood, picked up the bottle of Gusano Rojo and pushed

it with all of his strength into the Big Chief's face. The glass shattered and cut into Catalina's nose, cheeks, and chin. Romeo picked up the largest piece and stabbed both of the man's eyes, then jammed the jagged edge into his throat and tore it open. Blood gushed out of the Big Chief's face and neck, but he made no noise other than a slight gurgle before collapsing to the floor behind his desk. Romeo leaned over him and saw the mezcal worm lying on the floor. He picked up the worm and dropped it into Catalina's mouth.

'There you go, *macho*,' Romeo said. 'You've proved your manhood now.'

'We're not staying for dinner,' Romeo said as he took Estrellita's arm and lifted her to her feet. 'Come on, Perdita, Duane. I just heard the food here's not so good.'

Flight

Due to the powder burns, Woody Dumas had most of the left side of his head covered with a gauze bandage. Firing the gun so close to his face had left him at least temporarily deaf in his left ear. Woody was on a plane to Los Angeles, slumped in a window seat sipping orange juice, thinking about his life, which had almost been squeezed out of him by Provino 'The Fist' Momo in a Dallas alley.

It wasn't really so terrible, he figured. Look at the situation in Eastern Europe, where so many people are desperate to escape to the West, leaving behind them possessions, parents, even children in their feverish rush to freedom. Or in China, with the soldiers shooting students down like dogs in Tiananmen Square. The government here had done that, too, of course, back in the sixties, and the Mexicans murdered dozens in '68 before the Olympics. Person-to-person violence is never as horrifying as faceless, wholesale slaughter, Woody decided, not ultimately. As gruesome and senseless as some individual murders are, he thought, the impersonality of mass maiming and killing is sordid and perverse beyond belief.

Woody remembered an old guy named Buzzard who used to hang around the neighborhood when Woody was a kid. Buzzard was almost a bum, but not quite. He fixed zippers and did some sewing for people, so Woody figured he must have been a tailor at one time in his life. Buzzard always had about ten days' growth of whiskers sticking out of his long, mule-like face, and he walked around flapping his arms as if they were wings, which was why everyone called him Buzzard. He wore a red-and-black-checkered lumberjack coat that obviously had never been cleaned, and a blue peaked cap with earmuff flaps tied together on top. His eyes, Woody recalled, were clear green with black specks in them. Nobody knew where Buzzard slept until he was found poisoned to death in an unused trash bin behind the public library. He'd been drinking black liquid Shinola shoe polish, using a slice of Wonder bread as a filter, pouring the Shinola through the bread into a coffee can. The only other thing in the trash bin with Buzzard's body was a dog-eared hardcover copy of the 1914 A. L. Burt Company edition of *Tarzan of the Apes* by Edgar Rice Burroughs, which was tucked like a pillow under Buzzard's head.

A stewardess came by with a cart and said something to Woody. He turned his head so that he could listen with the good ear and asked her what she'd said.

'May I bring you another orange juice?' she asked.

'Sure, sure, I'd like that,' Woody said, handing her his plastic cup. Then he had another thought. 'Oh, miss? Could you please make this one a screwdriver?'

She nodded, refilled the cup with juice, and gave it back to Woody along with a miniature bottle of Wolfschmidt. He paid her, unscrewed the cap and poured the contents into the orange juice, mixing it around with the index finger of his right hand. Woody had not drunk an alcoholic beverage in nearly a decade and he wasn't certain why he'd decided to do so now; it just seemed like the right thing to do. Woody lifted the cup.

'For Buzzard,' he said.

Salamanders

Perdita didn't like what was happening. She was pleased to be going to Los Angeles, but she knew already that it was over between her and Romeo. She wouldn't say anything yet, just let the deal go down and pick her spot to split. Maybe take care of this Estrellita bitch before then.

'What's on your indecent little mind tonight, honey?' asked Romeo. 'You been awful quiet lately.'

Romeo and Perdita were at the Round-up Drive-in in Yuma, waiting at the take-away counter for their order. They'd left Duane and Estrellita tied up together back in the motel room.

'Nothin' much, tell the truth. Just appreciatin' the beautiful evenin'.'

Cars and trucks zoomed by on the street in front of the drive-in. The air was sickly warm and sticky and stank of burnt oil. A grayish haze hung like a soiled sheet across the sky. The breeze kicked at a corner of it now and again, wrinkling the gray just long enough to permit a peek at the twinkling platinum dots decorating the furious fuchsia. A tall, lean, cowboy-looking guy in his late twenties walked up to the take-out window.

'How you people doin' tonight?' he said.

'Not bad,' said Romeo. 'Yourself?'

The cowboy took off his black Stetson, reached into it and took out a half-empty pack of unfiltered Luckies. He offered it to Romeo and Perdita, both of whom declined, then shook one between his lips, flipped the pack back in and replaced the hat over his thick, tangled dark-brown hair.

'Can't complain,' he said, and pulled a book of matches from the left breast pocket of his maroon pearl buttoned shirt and lit the cigarette. He bent down a little and looked in the window.

'Hey, Betsy!' he called. 'How about a couple double-cheese-burgers and a side of chili and slaw.'

'Be a few minutes, Cal,' a woman shouted from within. 'You want any fries with that?'

'Why not?' said Cal. 'I'll take whatever you got to give, Betsy.'

The woman laughed and yelled back, 'Oh, hush! You know that bar talk don't cut it with me.'

Cal smiled and straightened up. He stood off to the side of the window away from Romeo and Perdita and puffed on the Lucky Strike.

'So what's doin' in Yuma these days?' asked Romeo.

Cal looked at him and said, 'That your Cherokee there, with the Texas plates?'

'That's right.'

'You all from Texas, then?'

'Right again.'

'Passin' through, I suppose.'

'You got it.'

'Headed for California, I bet. LA.'

'You're on the money tonight, cowboy.'

Cal laughed, took a last drag, and tossed away the butt.

'Not a whole lot to keep people here, I don't guess,' he said. 'It ain't the most excitin' city in the world.'

'Nothin' wrong with peace and quiet, that's what you want.'

'Ain't much of that here, either. Heat gets people mean, fries their brains and makes 'em dangerous. Tough on every livin' thing except salamanders.'

'Salamanders?' said Perdita.

'Yeah,' said Cal, 'you know, them lizards can withstand fire.'

An eighteen-wheeler downshifted and belched as it passed by, spewing a brown cloud of diesel smoke over the drive-in. Perdita coughed and turned away.

'Here's your order, sir,' Betsy said to Romeo from the window, shoving it through. 'Be $17.25.'

Betsy was a middle-aged Asian woman with badly bleached blond hair.

Romeo put a twenty down on the counter, picked up the bag, and said, 'Change is yours.'

''Preciate it and come back now. Yours is comin' up, handsome,' she said to Cal.

'I ain't goin' nowhere.'

'No kiddin',' she said, and laughed.

‘You folks take care now,’ Cal said to Romeo and Perdita.

‘Do our best,’ said Romeo. ‘You, too.’

Driving back to the motel, Perdita said, ‘You get a good look at that gal back there?’

‘You mean Betsy?’

‘Woman had the worst hair, Jesus. Never saw no Oriental person with blond hair before.’

‘Plenty more surprises where we’re headed, Perdita. Just you wait. I got big plans for us.’

She turned and stared at Romeo. He was grinning, confident, full of himself.

‘Don’t make me no promises you can’t keep,’ Perdita said. ‘There ain’t nothin’ worse for a woman than a man punks out on her. That happens, no tellin’ what she’ll do.’

‘I’ll keep this in mind, sweet thing,’ said Romeo, nodding and grinning, ‘I surely will.’

History Lesson

'E. T. Satisfy, is it? Hometown, Dallas.'

'Right the first time.'

The clerk looked up from the registration card across the desk and down at Ernest Tubb.

'How you mean to pay for this?'

'Cash,' said Ernest Tubb, handing the clerk a hundred dollar bill.

The clerk took it, examined both sides, went into another room for a minute, then came back and gave Ernest Tubb his change plus a receipt and a room key.

'You got 237. Upstairs and around to the right. Ice and soda pop machines by the staircase. Need more you holler.'

'I'm obliged.'

In the room the first thing he did was phone home.

'Glory Ann? It's me, Ernest Tubb.'

'Just where in Judas's country are you?' she asked. 'I been worried crazy!'

'Easy, woman. I'm at the Holiday on Madre Island. Got a lead in Larry Lee County that Estelle and Duane Orel mighta come down here. College kids on break partyin' both sides of the border. Heard about two were kidnapped a week ago. Might be them. I'm headed for Mextown soon's I hang up.'

'Kidnapped! Save Jesus! Rita Louise Samples is here with me now, and Marfa Acker's comin' back later. They been my cross and crutch since you disappeared on me.'

'I ain't disappeared. I told you, I'm huntin' for Estelle.'

'If I lose you, too, don't know what I'll do.'

'You ain't lost nothin', Glory, includin' weight. You stickin' to that lima bean diet Dr Breaux put you on?'

'Ernest Tubb, be serious! Who can think about dietin' at a time like this?'

'I am serious, Glory Ann. You keep eatin' like a herd of javelinas cut loose in a Arby's and you'll flat explode! Rita Louise and Marfa be scrapin' your guts off the kitchen walls and collectin' 'em in a box to bury. You keep clear of them coffeecakes, hear?'

Glory Ann began to cry.

'Oh, Ernest Tubb, you're just a mean tiny man.'

'Lima beans, Glory Ann, Lima beans,' he said, and hung up.

Ernest Tubb backed his Continental out of the parking space, drove to the motel lot exit and turned right. He was thinking about the last time he and Glory Ann had made love. She'd insisted on being on top and just about squashed him. He'd felt like he imagined those people in their cars felt when that freeway fell on them during the big quake in California.

It was several seconds before Ernest Tubb realized that he'd turned his Mark IV in the wrong direction on a one-way thoroughfare. By the time he saw the nose of the White Freightliner and heard the horn blast it was too late for him to do anything about it.

'Oh, Glory!' Ernest Tubb said, and then he was history.

Back at the Nursery

'You understand what has to be done?'

'I do.'

'You have no problem about it?'

Reggie hesitated, then shook his head no.

'Good.'

Santos poured more Glenmorangie into his glass, swirled the brown liquid around and stared down into it.

'You and your cousin have been close friends, have you not?'

'We were raised together as boys, but then Romeo and his mother left Caribe. Since then we are in touch.'

Santos took off his yellow-framed sunglasses and set them on the table. He rubbed his eyes with his abbreviated left hand, then smoothed back his hair. He looked at Reginald San Pedro Sula, who wanted to turn away from the two small darting animals imprisoned in Marcello's face, but Reggie steeled himself and did not flinch. Santos's eyes were the color of Christmas trees on fire.

'It's not that there is anything personal in this,' Santos said, 'but Romeo has done some terrible things, things so terrible that not even the Mexican authorities can allow him to operate there any longer. I have sent some people in to take care of the situation in Zopilote. From now on we will handle the business. It was necessary to remove your cousin from the area in order to effect the change. In the meantime, he does us the favor of transporting other goods for us, for which he is fairly compensated. After the delivery is secured, you will pay him the remainder of what we have agreed, and then you will kill him.'

Santos lifted his glass with the fingers and opposing digit of his right hand and drank most of the Scotch in it.

'After Romeo is dead, of course,' he said, 'the money is no good to him, so you will take it as payment for doing me this favor.'

'That is most generous of you,' said Reggie.

Santos closed his eyes and shook his head.

'Not generous, Reggie – just. There is a difference.'

He reopened his eyes and put his sunglasses back on. Reggie relaxed, taking off his powder-blue porkpie hat and wiping the sweat from his bald head with a lime-green handkerchief.

'Deception is merely a tool of resourcefulness,' said Santos. 'Have you ever heard of Captain Philippe Legorjus?'

'I don't believe so, sir.'

'Well, he is the commander of France's élite anti-terrorist forces. Not long ago he was sent by his government to New Caledonia, which is in the South Pacific, to quell an uprising by the Kanak rebels on the island of Ouvea. New Caledonia is part of the French Overseas Territories, and so it was necessary to protect the French citizens who live there. It is also the place from which the French conduct their nuclear tests.

'In any case, Captain Legorjus was kidnapped by the rebels, along with twenty-two others. The leader of the Kanak Socialist National Liberation Front, I believe it was called, was something of a religious fanatic, and had been trained for guerrilla warfare in Libya by Khadafy. This man vowed to maintain a state of permanent insecurity in the French South Pacific Territory if the separatists' demands for independence were not met. A familiar story. I remember a newspaper photograph of him, wearing a hood and holding a rifle, the pockets of his field jacket stuffed with cartridges. He threatened to kill a white person a day so long as the French government occupied Noumea, the capital of New Caledonia.

'While the Kanak leader carried on making speeches to the press, Legorjus organized the hostages and not only led them to freedom but took control of the separatist stronghold, disarmed the rebel soldiers, and captured their leader, enabling several hundred French naval infantrymen to swarm in and restore order. Upon his return to Paris, Legorjus was accorded a parade down the Champs d'Elysées and declared a national hero.'

Santos paused and looked at Reggie, who smiled and said, 'He must be a brave man, this captain.'

Santos nodded. 'Brave and cunning, Reggie. I make a point of studying these kinds of extraordinary men. There is much to be learned from their behavior. My firm belief is that life must be lived according to a man's own terms, or else it is probably not worth living.'

'I am sure you are right, Mr Santos.'

Marcello licked the stub on his left hand where his thumb had been.

'I know you will do a good job for me,' he said, walking over to the window and looking out at the sky.

'Ah, *si sta facendo scuro*,' Santos said. 'It's getting dark. You know, Reggie, I am almost seventy years old, and despite all I know, there is still nothing I can do about that.'

Waves

Woody looked out at the swimming pool. There were three kids and a dog in it, a golden retriever. Apparently the motel people didn't mind that the dog was swimming. He'd been in there for at least fifteen minutes and nobody had said anything about it. California was a different world, anyway, Woody thought. Maybe the animal rights group had successfully lobbied for legislation allowing dogs to use motel pools.

The Wild Palms Motel, where Woody Dumas was staying, was in the middle of Hollywood, one block south of Sunset. It was not the kind of place Woody thought he could ever get used to, let alone like. The weather was good enough, he supposed, but the people in LA had a way of talking that put him off. It was as if they were convinced everything they said either had a deeper meaning or meant something other than what Woody thought they were saying. Maybe it was the spectre of the film industry that made everyone want to feel as if they belonged in it, like a club, and were therefore integral to the machinery of the place. He couldn't quite put his finger on it, but whatever it was, Woody didn't get it.

Not that it mattered, anyway. Woody was in town to do a job, and tonight he would be staked out across the street from a warehouse on Ivar just off Hollywood Boulevard, a few blocks from the Wild Palms, awaiting the arrival of a shipment of illicit skin. According to the best information available to the various authorities, Crazy Eyes Santos was operating cosmetics factories on the West Coast, using wetbacks to do most of the work. Seizing a delivery of the proportion expected tonight or tomorrow would be a major step in cracking the operation.

Woody decided to have lunch and then come back to the motel and take a nap. He walked past the swimming pool on the way to his car and noticed a beautiful young woman sitting in a lounge chair dedicatedly applying suntan lotion to herself. She had long blond hair, a slender figure and very long legs. She wore an orange, tiger-striped bikini and oversized blue sunglasses, the frames of which were shaped like butterfly wings. The golden retriever had his paws up on the side of the pool in front of the young woman and was barking excitedly in her direction. A terrifically fat man wearing a pair of lavender Bermuda shorts and nothing else to cover his vast, very pale expanse of skin, came out and jumped into the pool, displacing no small amount of water, most of which splashed on the young woman, disturbing her ministrations.

'Marv, you fat piece of pigshit!' she screamed, jumping up. 'Did you have to do that?!'

The golden retriever clambered out of the pool and shook himself furiously right next to her.

'Goddammit!' she said, throwing her plastic bottle of lotion at the dog, somehow missing him by a good six feet. 'This is going to be a great fucking time!'

Woody continued to the parking lot, unlocked the government K-car, got in and started it. He decided to drive out to Santa Monica, to the ocean. It might be nice, Woody thought, to buy a sandwich and sit and look at the water for a while.

He'd eaten half of a BLT and was sipping from a can of Canada Dry ginger ale through a straw, when a tall, gaunt-faced man who looked to be in his mid-forties, sat down on the bench next to Woody. The tall man, Woody thought, resembled the actor John Carradine, but a beaten-down, hard-luck version; more the way Carradine looked as the ex-preacher in the movie of *The Grapes of Wrath*. The man's clothes were shabby, worn-out, and he needed a shave, but he held himself erect and gave the appearance of being at ease.

'Do you mind if I speak to you?' the man said.

'No,' said Woody.

The man stared at Woody and examined the gauze bandages. His eyes were black, without light. When he spoke, Woody noticed that several of his teeth were missing.

'You've been injured.'

'Burned,' Woody said.

'I hope you're not too uncomfortable.'

'I'm doing fine, thanks.'

The man turned his face back toward the ocean.

'Waves are the heartbeat of the earth,' he said.

'That's not bad,' said Woody. 'I like that.'

'I used to be a poet. A singer, too, in nightclubs. I sang the songs I wrote. But no longer.'

'Why'd you stop?'

'You probably think I'm an alcoholic, or a drug addict, but I'm not. I like to have a martini now and then, of course, and I've sampled drugs, but they're not to blame for my condition, which, as you can see, is less than glamorous. I just lost interest in life, that's what happened. There's nobody to blame, not even myself. I'm not crazy, either. At least I don't think I am. One day the carriage stopped for me and I waved it on.'

'Are you hungry?' Woody asked. 'You can have this half of my sandwich, if you like.'

The man took the sandwich from Woody and held it in his lap.

'You're very gracious,' he said. 'Are you a religious person?'

'Not really, no.'

'Neither am I, never have been. Organized religion is unseemly.'

'Here, you can have the rest of this, too,' said Woody, handing the man the can of ginger ale.

Woody stood up. 'I've got to go.'

'I know, your carriage is here.'

Woody laughed. 'I suppose it is.'

'You understand,' said the man, 'it's not as if I had no choice.'

'I believe you,' Woody said, watching the man bite into the sandwich.

Camisado

'Hey, buddy, it's been a long time!'

'Too long, I guess.'

Doug Fakaofo and Romeo hugged each other and smiled.

'I was glad to hear you were comin' out,' said Doug. 'What brings you?'

'Business, what else these days, huh? Not that we can't put in some good party time, too, of course,' laughed Romeo.

'That's great, man!'

'But I got a favor to ask you, Doug. I got some people with me and I want to leave 'em here while I take care of something. It shouldn't take long, maybe only a couple of hours. We're just in off the road and they'll prob'ly sleep for a while anyway.'

'Hey, you know it's no problem. They'll be safe here. Bring 'em into the house.'

'Thanks, man. I knew I could count on you.'

'Any time.'

Romeo had spoken to Lily Fakaofo, Doug's wife, from a pay phone in El Centro. Doug was out at the time, but Lily had told Romeo they'd be happy to see him. The Fakaofos lived in Hacienda Heights, a largely Samoan-American section of Los Angeles. The Samoan community was a tight one, distrustful of mainstream America; they kept mostly to themselves. Not even the police knew much about the people there, and Romeo figured it would be a perfect place to stash Estrellita and Duane while he and Perdita delivered the shipment to Reggie in Hollywood.

Doug 'Big Brown' Fakaofo had been in the Marines with Romeo, and they'd kept in touch. The Fakaofos were heavy reefer users and they greatly appreciated the kilos Romeo sent them via UPS from Texas on their birthdays and at Christmastime. Both Doug and Lily were large individuals, Doug going about two-eighty and Lily a nifty two-ten or so. Lily's brother, Tutu

Nukuono, whom Romeo had met only once, weighed well over three hundred pounds. Tutu had worked as a plumber with Doug until a few months before, when he beat a cop to death with a chain during a brawl in the parking lot of the Moonlight Lagoon, a local bar that catered mainly to Pacific islanders. Tutu was now serving a life sentence without possibility of parole at Folsom.

'I sure was sorry to hear about your brother, Lily,' Romeo said. 'He's a good kid.'

Lily shrugged. 'He shoulda known better than to stomp a uniform. Him and a bunch of his biker buddies got carried away wailin' on some Devil's Dragons, I guess it was, who'd strayed into the neighborhood.'

'White boys lookin' for strange-colored pussy,' said Doug. 'They got into it with Tutu's gang, the cops come, one of the blues tangled with Tutu, and that was it. Only reason he didn't get the gas was there weren't no way they could prove premeditation.'

'Well, I know Folsom ain't no picnic,' said Romeo.

Doug nodded. 'Yeah, but Tutu already got himself some friends inside. Anybody can handle it, he will. Let's go get your people.'

Lily told Romeo she'd feed Duane and Estrellita, then lock them in the back bedroom, the one Tutu had used. Doug volunteered to ride shotgun for Romeo in the truck; Perdita would follow them in the Cherokee and they'd all drive back together to Hacienda Heights.

'She's some tough, sexy-lookin' lady, that Perdita,' Doug said to Romeo as they headed off to deliver the goods.

Romeo grinned. 'Think she's a keeper, do ya?'

Doug laughed. 'Guess I could keep her occupied for a hour or few, I concentrated hard enough,' he said.

'Never doubted you for a minute, Big Brown. Perdita Durango's somethin' all right. Picked her up at a fruitshake stand in New Orleans. The creature's got a mind of her own, though, you know?'

'Just have to be sure she don't stay awake longer'n you do, she's angry about somethin''. Some women you need to watch like that. Lily's on my side all the way, always has been.'

'You're a lucky fellow, Doug. Stay that way.'

'Tryin' to. What you plan to do with those kids?'

'It's a good question. Think we've squeezed just about all the use out of 'em. They've seen too much to cut loose. I'll deal with that pretty quick, soon as this is finished.'

Romeo kept checking in the sideview for Perdita. She stayed right behind them all the way. When Romeo brought the truck to a stop in front of the warehouse on Ivar, Perdita drove the Cherokee past it and parked a half-block up the street. Doug and Romeo got out and Romeo walked over and knocked on the side door of the building.

'*Hola, primo!* You made it OK, I see,' said Reggie, after opening the door. 'Come on in.'

'I have a friend with me. This is Doug Fakaofo. You remember I told you about him, Reggie. "Big Brown." He was with me in Beirut.'

'Of course,' Reggie said, shaking hands with Doug. 'Come in.'

As soon as the door closed, Woody Dumas got out of the K-car and motioned with his right arm to the men on the roof of the building next to the warehouse. At that moment, a dozen vehicles, carrying both federal and local law enforcement personnel, converged on the street, entering from either end. Two men used a battering ram on the door, which easily gave way, and most of the rest of them, led by Woody Dumas, ran in single file.

Woody saw Reginald San Pedro Sula, dressed in a blue denim leisure suit and wearing a Los Angeles Dodgers baseball cap, fire two rounds from a .45 automatic; the first into the forehead of Romeo Dolorosa, the second into the left temple of Doug Fakaofo, killing each of them instantly.

'Federal agents!' Woody shouted, as the men surrounded the shooter.

Reggie dropped the gun and raised his hands. He started to smile, but before he could complete it several men grabbed him and threw him to the ground, causing his head to bang against the concrete floor. Woody knelt by the men who had been shot, verifying that they were dead. The forehead wound in the smaller of the two looked large enough for a decent-sized sewer rat to crawl through. The man's mouth was open and Woody could not help but be impressed by his extraordinarily large, perfectly formed teeth that even in death radiated a powerful white light.

After Hours

Lily Fakaofo was up late, sitting at the kitchen table reading the newspaper, listening to the 24-hour news station on the radio, smoking a cigarette and working her way through the second box of Nilla Wafers she'd eaten since Doug, Romeo, and Perdita had left two and a half hours before. Estrellita and Duane were asleep in Tutu's room.

'From Harare, Zimbabwe, comes this story,' said the radio. 'The Zimbabwe Football Association banned four players for life yesterday for publicly urinating on the field at a Harare soccer stadium. Association chairman Nelson Chirwa said the organization was appalled by the behavior last Sunday of the four players of the southern Tongogara team. "It is a public indecency for a player to openly urinate on the football pitch," Chirwa said. "We all know that it is all superstition and that the belief in juju that almost all the clubs have taken to believe in is strongly deplored by the association." He said the four were advised to urinate on the field by witch doctors, who said it would ensure a victory. It didn't. Tongogara lost, two to nothing.'

Lily laughed and took a puff on her Bel-Air Menthol Slim. Doug had told her that he thought Romeo Dolorosa was mixed up with some kind of voodoo cult down in Mexico or Texas, but she didn't want to know about it. There was enough real mysterious shit going down in the world, Lily thought, without getting sucked into that phony black magic crap. Take this strange business in Russia she was reading about.

A forty-two-year-old French-Armenian multimillionaire art dealer, who was also a well-known poet, had disappeared in Moscow five months ago. He'd been having a meeting with three Soviet business associates in his hotel room near Red Square when he received a telephone call. He spoke briefly to the caller, hung up, and told his associates to wait there, that he had to go out but would return within the hour. They saw him get into a black Zhiguli limousine and speed away, and that's the last anyone had seen or heard of him, including his family in Paris.

Police, KGB agents, and the Soviet government, specifically the Visual Arts Department of the Cultural Affairs Ministry, with whom he'd had dealings for several years, were pursuing the case. Speculation was that with the restructuring of the Soviet society and increasing entrepreneurial climate, the art dealer had engaged in unlawful export of Russian Orthodox icons and other art items in league with the various crime organizations operating throughout the Soviet Union. Authorities in Moscow were paying particularly close attention to the case because of their feeling that it could lead to the exposure of a homegrown Mafia.

According to an official in the Department of Cultural Affairs, this art dealer was a clever man who spoke several languages fluently, had a wide variety of friends in many countries, was very confident and thought there was nothing he couldn't handle. He had made his millions in a very short period of time, a decade or so, having started out with next to nothing in a small Paris gallery. His family were convinced that he had no dealings with gangsters.

Those involved in the investigation theorized that the art dealer had become enmeshed in a power struggle among the seven major Moscow Mafia families, and found himself in a situation he could not handle; or, that he had simply been double-crossed and disposed of. Another rumor circulating in Armenia and Paris held that he had been selling artworks to the Soviet government itself, that a number of the items were revealed to be forgeries, and he had been killed by the KGB, who dumped his body in a forest outside Moscow. This version maintained that the body had been discovered five days after his disappearance, and the family was fostering the pretense that they had heard nothing from or about him in an effort not to discredit the gallery or his reputation. It was, therefore, a mystery that might never be solved.

'Ha!' said Lily, turning the page. 'Another hotshot too smart for his own good.'

Lily wolfed down another Nilla Wafer and stretched her back. She figured Doug might stay out partying with Romeo and Perdita after they'd delivered whatever it was they had, and she was thinking that she might just as well go to bed, when the radio brought her up short.

'In Hollywood tonight, a gun battle left two men dead and resulted in the capture of another by federal drug agents, the FBI and the Los Angeles County Sheriff's Department. An illegal cosmetics factory, specializing in the use of unauthorized products and operated in central Hollywood by organized crime, was raided at midnight during a delivery of approximately one solid ton of human placentas. Authorities identified the dead men as Romeo Dolorosa, of Tampa, Florida, and Douglas Fakaofo, of Los Angeles. The man taken into custody was identified as Reginald San Pedro Sula, a citizen of the Central American republic of Caribe. All of the men are suspected members of the crime family headed by Marcello "Crazy Eyes" Santos, which is based in New Orleans, Louisiana, and Dallas, Texas. According to Drug Enforcement Special Agent Woodrow W. Dumas, who led the raid, seizure of the two thousand pound shipment of placentas, used in the manufacture of anti-aging skin creams, and discovery of the illegal plant is a major breakthrough. More arrests are expected. Well, folks, that's another kind of Hollywood skin factory, isn't it?'

Lily dropped both her cigarette and the cookie she'd just taken from the box and stood up, knocking over her chair. She rushed to the rear bedroom, unlocked the door and flipped on the light.

'Get up! Get up now!' she screamed at Estrellita and Duane, who were huddled together on the bed. 'Get up and get out! Get out of the house! Go, go!'

Estrellita and Duane ran out into the night, taking off down the street as fast as they could. Lily collapsed on the floor of Tutu's room.

'Doug!' she cried. 'Doug, you big brown dummy! You poor, big, beautiful, dead dummy! What's your ugly old Samoan mama Lily gonna do now?'

Late Date

As soon as Frankie Toro spotted the woman he pulled his metallic cherry Lexus to the curb, leaned over and lowered the window on the passenger side. She was leaning against a mud-encrusted black Jeep parked in the space closest to the street in the lot of an Oki-Dog on Santa Monica Boulevard, holding a soft drink cup and smoking a cigarette.

This was easily the hottest-looking chick Frankie Toro had seen that night. Twenty-two or three, he figured, about five-six, a hundred and ten, hard body, shiny black hair almost to her ass, skin like *café con leche*. A genuine *chicana* doll. She reminded Frankie of Tura Sultana, that steel-cheekboned, *nagual*-eyed, Japanese-Cherokee leather bitch he'd seen in Russ Meyer's desert chase tit movie, *Faster Pussycat, Kill! Kill!*

'Hey, *guapita,*' Frankie yelled to her, 'you want a date?'

Perdita picked up her bag and slung it over her left shoulder, then walked slowly to the Lexus and looked at the grinning, eager idiot. She smiled at him, stretching the cobras. Frankie pushed open the door.

'Been dyin' for you to ask,' she said, and slid in.

Light in the Forest

'Mama?'

'Estelle? Is that you? This is Rita Louise.'

'Oh, Mrs Samples. Is my mama there?'

'No, honey, no, she's down at the funeral home, makin' the arrangements. She's been out of her mind worried about you. Where've you been? Are you all right?'

'What arrangements, Mrs Samples? Why's she at a funeral home?'

'Oh, my word, Estelle. Of course, you wouldn't know.'

'Know what? What wouldn't I know?'

'Your daddy, Estelle, honey. Ernest Tubb. He got kilt in a car crash on Madre Island. The body just arrived today.'

'Car crash? Daddy's gone?'

Estelle dropped the phone, fell to the floor of the booth and fainted dead away.

'Estelle? Estelle, are you there?' Rita Louise's voice jumped out of the dangling receiver.

Duane half-lifted Estelle with his right arm and put the telephone to his left ear.

'Mrs Samples? It's Duane Orel. Estelle's sorta passed out here. Just tell Glory Ann we're safe now, we got away, and if she could to please wire us the airfare to come home.'

'I will, Duane, of course, but where are you?'

'Los Angeles, California, ma'am. Western Union downtown'll do. We'll head there soon as Estelle comes to. We been hidin' in the bushes all night.'

'Goodness, Duane, isn't life a mess sometimes.'

'Yes, ma'am. You'll pardon me sayin' this, but shit happens.'

The Old Testament

Santos hung up but kept his right hand on the telephone. He groaned and pressed his lips tightly together.

'Bad news, huh, Marcello?'

He sat back in a leather armchair and looked through his dark glasses across the room at Mona Costatroppo, who was perched on a white satin loveseat, her freshly shaved and lotioned legs tucked back under her spreading rump. She had on a low-cut black dress and a single strand of pearls that Santos had bought for her at Cartier in New York. They had cost him nine thousand dollars, Marcello recalled. Mona had a drink in one hand, an unlit black cigarette in the other. She always had a drink in her hand, Santos thought.

'*Una pioggia continua*,' he said.

'What now?'

'What now? Now is as before. All fucked up. First, it was Dede. Then *Il Pugno*, The Fist, who we send to hit and who himself gets hit. Now, Reggie, along with the West Coast factory.'

'Who Reggie? You mean the *tutsun* from Puerto Rico?'

'Caribe, not Puerto Rico. Caribe.'

Mona swallowed a mouthful of gin.

'You drink too much,' said Santos. 'You're getting fat, too.'

'Like Lina, you mean,' Mona said. 'You got a fat wife, you don't want a fat girlfriend, too, huh? You gonna dump me, Marcello? Is that what you want to do?'

Santos removed his hand from the phone, formed it like a gun, with the third finger and pinkie folded back, the thumb up, and the index and second fingers pointed at Mona. She froze.

'Bang,' he said.

Back from Eternity

'Hear you had a good trip.'

'Don't know about good, Doyle. Successful, anyway. We got what we went for. That LA is a whole other state of mind, though.'

'Didn't lose anyone, either, they tell me.'

'No white hats, but I woulda preferred to've brought in the delivery boys. Santos's trigger man took 'em both out before we got there.'

'Why you suppose they whacked Dolorosa?'

'Santos set him up. Crazy Eyes controls the border and Dolorosa got the area freaked out with his *santería* routine. Killing the boy was the last straw far as Santos was concerned.'

'Kidnapped two college kids, too. They turned up in LA, you know that?'

'Only heard about it after I got back to Dallas. What'd they have to say about Perdita Durango?'

'Didn't want to talk about her much, just said she's plenty weird and dangerous. They're pretty shook. The girl's father was killed in a car wreck while she was gone, which doesn't help. Happened while he was out huntin' for her, apparently.'

'That's rough, all right. What's her name?'

'Satisfy. Estelle Kenedy Satisfy. His is Duane Orel King.'

'That Satisfy sounds familiar, but I can't place it just now.'

'Well, Woodrow, I got to run. Hell of a job, bud.'

'*Gracias*, señor.'

'Oh, by the way, how's your hearing?'

'Back in stereo.'

'*Bueno*. Be talkin' to ya.'

59° and Raining in Tupelo

Tattooed on the bicep of Shorty's left arm were the words ONE LIFE ONE WIFE and tattooed on his right bicep was the name CHERRY ANN.

'That her?' Perdita asked him.

'Who?' said Shorty.

'Cherry Ann your wife's name?'

'Was.'

'She change it?'

Shorty laughed and shook his head no.

'Changed wives,' he said.

'Kinda puts the lie to your other arm, don't it?'

Shorty yawned and closed his eyes. He opened them and picked up his glass and took a long swallow of Pearl.

'Ain't nothin' stays similar, sweetheart, let alone the same. Or ain't you figured that out yet?'

Perdita Durango and Shorty Dee were sitting on adjacent stools at the bar of Dottie's Tupelo Lounge. It was eight-thirty on Friday night, December thirtieth. Oklahoma State was playing Wyoming in the Sea World Holiday Bowl football game on the television set above the bar.

'Know what I like to watch more than anything else?' Shorty said.

'Not knowin' you any better than I do, which is not at all practically,' said Perdita, 'I'd be afraid to ask.'

'Punt returns.'

'That so.'

'Yeah. Some people it's triples. Me it's punt returns. I like any kind of runbacks: kickoffs, interceptions, fumbles. But there's somethin' special about a little jackrabbit of a guy takin' a tall ball and turnin' on his jets.'

Shorty took another sip of beer.

'You been in town long?' he asked.
'Few days.'
'How's it goin' so far?'
'Been rainin' since I got here. Weather always like this?'
'Time of year it is. Fifty-nine and rainin' sounds about right for Christmas.'
'What else Tupelo got to offer?'
'Other than bein' the birthplace of Elvis Presley, you mean?'
Perdita laughed. She swept back her long, straight black hair with one hand and picked up her glass with the other.
'Didn't know about Elvis bein' born in Miss'ippi,' she said, and took a sip of beer.
'Where you from?' asked Shorty.
'Here and there. Texas, mostly.'
'Brings you this way?'
'Lookin' for somethin', I guess.'
Shorty offered his right hand.
'Shorty Dee. Glad to be of service if I can.'
She squeezed his fingers.
'Perdita Durango. Pleased to meet you, Shorty. You still married?'
Shorty laughed. 'Thought we was beginnin' a conversation here.'
Perdita smiled. 'How about buyin' me a new beer?'
'Now you're talkin', honey,' he said, signaling for another round. 'Got any more potentially embarrassin' questions you want to get out of the way?'
'You rich?'
The bartender set two more bottles on the bar in front of them.
Shorty laughed again. 'Nigger rich, maybe,' he said.
'Bein' nigger rich is all right, I guess,' said Perdita, 'long as a body got enough friends is rich for damn sure.'
They picked up the fresh bottles of beer and tapped them together.
'There you go,' said Shorty.
Perdita smiled. 'Here I go,' she said.